We went to the fam her own soda fountain for entertaining. She took a quart of chocolate-chocolate chip out of the freezer, filled two bowls with it, spooned on fudge sauce and chocolate sprinkles and topped it all off with real whipped cream and a maraschino cherry. Pig heaven!

"Now theoretically," Paula said with her mouth full, "you shouldn't want this. Superstrong aversion."

I sat there looking at the sundae, waiting for the post-hypnotic suggestions to take over but no mysterious voice welled up inside me to help me refrain.

"No aversion," I said. "Let's see what happens if I just taste it. Maybe it will start then."

I picked up my spoon and tasted the sundae. When I next came up for for air, my dish was empty.

"It certainly isn't working yet," Paula said.

Available from Crosswinds

The Eye of the Storm
by Susan Dodson

Sylvia Smith-Smith
by Peter Nelson

The Gifting
by Ann Gabhart

Bigger is Better

SHEILA SCHWARTZ

CROSSWINDS

New York • Toronto
Sydney • Auckland
Manila

In Gratitude: Andrea Brown, Agent
Elizabeth Schwartz, Research
Carolyn Marino, Editor

"Provide, Provide" from *The Poetry of Robert Frost* edited
by Edward Connery Lathem.
Copyright 1936 by Robert Frost. Copyright © 1964 by Lesley
Frost Ballantine. Copyright © 1969 by Holt, Rinehart and
Winston. Also full acknowledgement to the Estate of Robert
Frost and Jonathan Cape Limited.

First publication October 1987

ISBN 0-373-98009-4

SHEILA SCHWARTZ successfully combines at least two careers. She is an award-winning professor of education and adolescent literature at the State University College in New Paltz, New York, and she is a best-selling author. Her published work includes an adult novel, *The Solid Gold Circle*, and a novel for young adults, *Like Mother, Like Me*, which was adapted for television. Dr. Schwartz grew up in New York City.

Chapter One

These are the main things my best friend Paula and I have in common: we're both fat, we both have celebrity mothers and we wish people would stop bothering us about our weight.

Shortly after my sixteenth birthday, we were lying on chaises next to my pool, listening to Bruce Springsteen and stuffing on Poppycock.

"Oh, God," Paula said, "he's so intense."

"I know, I love him," I answered. "He's the love of my life. I'll never forgive him for getting married."

"A friend of mine says he lives up in the Hollywood Hills," Paula said.

"You mean at this very moment the passion of my life may be only twenty minutes away from me?"

"Yeah! But with his new wife."

"Far out! Call your friend and find out his address. We'll drive by and maybe we'll see him. I'd absolutely freak out."

"Okay. Let's go cruise. My friend lives in Beachwood Canyon. Maybe he'll be home."

We were struggling up out of our chaises when my beautiful mother, Sharon Long, the movie star, came clicking out on her high heels. She always wears high heels. She wears them on the beach, mountain climbing and at home. Her bedroom slippers have high heels. If she jogged, she'd jog in high heels. She says she's more comfortable in them, but that's not the main reason. High heels always make legs look better. That's why ballerinas stand on point.

In addition to high heels, she was wearing a Princess Stephanie bathing suit and new Revo sunglasses. Clasped in her hands with their long, perfect nails was the *L.A. Times*.

"Just a minute, you two," she said in that low, throaty voice that was familiar to millions. "Have you seen this?"

She shook the paper at us.

"Sure," I teased her, "it's the *L.A. Times*. I see it every day." Frankly I was a little surprised to see her clutching the front part of the paper. Usually she only reads the "Arts and Entertainment" section or the "Calendar" on weekends.

"We only get it on Sundays," Paula added. "My mother says it comes off all over her hands. What's up? An earthquake?"

"Get serious, you two!" Sharon's voice sank one octave to melodrama range. "Something tragic is about to happen that will affect the rest of your time in school."

"Mom, you know I don't believe those astrological columns."

She lit a cigarette in a long holder that she had bought from the estate of some thirties star and said, "Not another word until you listen to this article."

We both let out groans that she quelled with a stern glance. "It's at moments like these," she said, but she softened her words with a grin, "that I understand why Joan Crawford was so mean to her kids."

We both sat quietly and listened while she read the article from that day's paper.

It said that some state bigwigs had decided too many California students were out of shape and were naming several school districts to participate in an experimental program that would include more physical education, expanded health tests and improved nutrition of cafeteria food.

Sharon finished reading and looked at us. "Now will you two believe that this is serious?"

I shivered at the thought of a public discussion of my weight. "Maybe they won't get to our school, Mom."

"But suppose they do?"

"You mean they're going to come to classrooms and take us out if we're fat, the way reading teachers used to take kids out in elementary school? Or make us wear identifying armbands? What an embarrassment."

"That's right," Sharon said, lighting another cigarette. "A very public embarrassment. When they come to Beverly Hills High School with scads of photographers, which fat kids do you think they're going to photograph? Naturally, the kids of celebrities. I can just see the story. 'Charter members of the program are Lois Long, daughter of movie star Sharon Long, and Paula Lawrence, daughter of retired opera singer Rosetta

Lawrence.' The public will laugh at me and the other kids will laugh at you. I just can't bear to think of it.''

She looked at me and blinked back a few tears. Behind her mask of self-assurance and beauty and control, Sharon is really a kindhearted and concerned mother.

"Don't worry, Mom," I tried to joke. "Maybe I'll die before September. Maybe the world will destruct.''

"Nothing's going to happen to the world before next September. It's smarter to lose some weight than to wait for the end of the world.''

"Mom, I've tried to diet a million times in the past. You know that! I can't stay on a diet. I'm hungry all the time and I love to eat. And I hate exercise. It's a lost cause. Maybe I should join the circus as the fat lady.''

"I'm not going to let some police state force me to lose weight," Paula said indignantly. "My mother will sue. *She's* fat and she thinks it's nobody else's business. She says my fat is baby fat and I'll lose it in the next few years.''

"But it's different for her," Sharon pointed out. "She's no longer in the public eye, but I still have my career and photographers to worry about. The reason you two are overweight is that you lie around all day eating junk food. Everybody would like to do that. But smart women don't. They discipline themselves. Exercise plus diet. Diet plus exercise. That's all there is to it.''

"I've tried," I repeated. "Nothing worked.''

"Just because it didn't work before doesn't mean you should never try again. I don't believe either one of you ever tried hard enough. It's all a question of commitment. You have to give your all. Beauty knows no pain!

You have to keep saying that to yourself over and over again. Beauty knows no pain.''

She counted off on her fingers. "May, June, July, August. Four months to get thin before you go back to school. So what do you say? It's that or join the fat girls' class at school.''

I sighed, feeling the old, familiar depression creeping over me. It wasn't as if I hadn't tried before. I'd tried all kinds of diets, but nothing worked. I was as unalterably fat as a basketball star is unalterably six foot six.

"I'll try." I shrugged gloomily. "I really will, Mom. But I've never been able to stay on a diet even until lunchtime before this.''

"It's never too late. I believe in you." She blew us a kiss, then click-clacked back into the house.

It's a terrible burden to have a parent believe in you when you don't believe in yourself. Double disappointment every time.

"Let's go to the Beverly Center," I said to Paula after a while. Bopping around malls always makes me feel better and this one has twelve movie theaters and dozens of fast-food restaurants.

Chapter Two

We walked into Sharon's wing of the house to get some money. Missy, Sharon's longtime friend, live-in secretary and general girl Friday, was working at her desk with Marty, Sharon's agent. Sometimes my home seems like Grand Central Station. Among the people who come regularly, and honestly I'm not exaggerating, are Sharon's lawyer, agent, accountant, manicurist, pedicurist, hairstylist, voice coach, makeup man, exercise man, masseuse, nutritionist, astrologist and dressmaker. And every one of them seems to be personally offended by my weight.

Marty was chomping away on a big, black, fat, air-polluting cigar. "Aha! The beef trust! What are you girls going to do about all that weight?"

"We've decided to keep it," Paula said haughtily.

"Funny kid!" He glared at her.

"We need some money, Missy," I said.

"Would you believe the way these kids are brought up expecting handouts, Marty? I never got anything for nothing. I worked from the time I was six. I never had a free ride."

"What kind of job did you have when you were six?" Paula asked.

"I helped my parents in their little grocery store."

Marty blew out a cloud of cigar smoke, and Paula began to cough and wave at the air.

"Whadaya gonna do?" he said. "All these Beverly Hills kids are spoiled rotten. I should have their problems."

"Please give me some money," I repeated. "I obviously can't get a job this afternoon."

"You already had your allowance this week. Money does not grow on trees. In case you haven't noticed, your mother has not worked in eight months."

"Come on, Paula," I said. "We'll ask my mom."

"She acts as if she has to protect Sharon from you," Paula whispered as we walked to Sharon's exercise room.

"I know! Sick, isn't it?"

Sharon's exercise room is like a regular gym with a number of Nautilus machines and a Pilates table on which she works with Flash, her instructor, for an hour every day. The Pilates table is made of leather and straps and pulleys and closely resembles an ancient torture machine. It also closely resembles a modern torture machine. You lie on it and put your feet in the stirrups and do exercises like push-ups in a horizontal position. I've resisted trying it, but Sharon says it's great for muscle tone.

"Mom, would you please tell Missy to give us some money for the Beverly Center?" I asked as we walked in. "She's giving us a hard time."

Flash shivered at the sight of us and went into a big, exaggerated horror act that maybe he thought was funny. "Oh, my God, Sharon! She looks worse every time I see her." (Usually he comes when I'm in school.) "Put her on the cocaine diet. Send her to a fat farm. Sweetie, in this town only Chicanos are fat."

"I hate racist remarks," I said.

"I hate fat," he answered.

"Haven't you heard?" he continued. "Everybody normal is anorexic or bulimic. Honestly, I could weep." He shuddered and rolled his eyes toward heaven in dismay. He was so perturbed at our undisciplined weight that he took a diet soda out of the room's little refrigerator and lit a cigarette.

Paula and I looked at each other. We both hate smoking. Her mother won't even stay in a room with smokers. She says it hurts her voice.

"Don't worry, sweetie," he told Sharon. "I won't cut you short. I have extra time today. My next client is spending a month in Transylvania."

"Transylvania?" I asked. That really fascinated me. "You mean like where Dracula lived?"

"I don't know who lived there," he said, "but right now Madame Sikorsky lives there, and she has the most famous rejuvenation salon behind the Iron Curtain. They're noted for wrapping and sheep entrails."

"Wrapping nails?" I asked.

"Don't be dense. You can get your nails wrapped on every street in L.A. Body wrapping. They wrap the bodies tightly, like mummies, and immerse them in their local mineral water. It shrinks the fat and makes it compact."

"They wrap them like mummies while they're alive?" Paula asked in shock.

"What is it with these two?" he asked Sharon. "Are they retards as well as fat? Of course while they're alive. Why would dead people need to be thin?"

"I don't know." Paula giggled. "Maybe to get into heaven."

I also started to giggle. "What about the sheep entrails? You mean they burn them and pray to get thin, like in ancient Greece?"

"Of course not, dumdum. This is behind the Iron Curtain. They're not religious there. I think it's against the law or something. They make a little incision in the back and put in pills made of sheep entrails. They have two-week pills and one-month pills. Just a little incision, two stitches, and voila."

"Gross," Paula and I said together. "Sick."

Sharon got off the table and lit a cigarette. "Flash, honey," she said, "why don't you work with Lois?"

"Not if you cross my palm with gold, sweetie. I'm not into failure. She'd have to come fifty percent of the way, and I don't see her doing it. She'd have to show me first that she could lose some weight. Lois, baby, it's all very simple. You wouldn't weigh so much if you watched what goes into your mouth."

Paula has a very short fuse. I tend to be placid, which is why we complement each other so well. "And you wouldn't be so rude," she snapped at him, "if you watched what came out of yours. The two of you are sitting there smoking away. My mother wouldn't touch a cigarette. It's bad for the voice and, in case you haven't heard, smoking causes cancer.

"Personally," Paula continued, "I think women are being conned with all this thin business. I like the way my mother looks. Soft and warm! Why does everybody have to look like a bag of bones with a wig?"

"Sour grapes, sweetie. Even opera singers are thin nowadays. Hey, did you hear the latest fat joke?"

"I don't like jokes about fat people," I told him pointedly. "I don't like jokes about any people who are different. I think it's disgusting to build a career on someone else's fat."

"Careful there, sweetie," he said, "you're treading on my bread and butter."

I changed the subject. "So can we have some money?"

"How about getting some exercise first? You two have to stop being couch potatoes. Go out and swim some laps. Go out and run," Sharon said.

"Mom, we did swim today."

"I swam a lap," Paula protested.

"Two," I echoed weakly.

"Stop shining me on. Neither one of you has done anything today but walk back and forth to the refrigerators. Besides, one lap doesn't do any good. You have to swim a mile for it to matter."

"We'll get exercise walking around the Beverly Center."

She burst into laughter. "The only exercise you two get there is walking from food stand to food stand, sampling all along the way."

"Sweetie," Flash said, grinding out his cigarette. "Let the little piggies go. I'm ready."

"All right," she said, "ask Missy for twenty dollars. I'm figuring out a plan for your weight. These are your last days of freedom, so go and enjoy."

Chapter Three

Let's drive past my house and I'll get my money,"
Paula said. "That fruitcake has some nerve being so
judgmental."

"I suppose it's even better to be a fruitcake than to be
fat," I said. "I'm real depressed, Paula, about what's
going to happen in school. Maybe the school superin-
tendent will make us carry little bells like lepers in the
Middle Ages, and before we enter a class we'll have to
ring the bells and call out, 'Unclean! Unclean!'"

"It all makes me so mad," Paula said. "In this town,
image is all that matters. It's better to be a blond Bar-
bie doll with thin thighs, even if you have a bubble brain
and a valley-girl accent. Well, my mom will cheer us
up."

As we approached Paula's house, we could hear the
magnificent strains of her mother's voice wafting out to

us. "'Ride of the Valkyries,'" Paula said. I could feel my skin prickle at the sound.

Even though Mrs. Lawrence has retired from the opera stage, she still practices every day and does an occasional benefit concert. I adore listening to her. It absolutely amazes me that anybody can make such extraordinary sounds. Sharon hates the opera, which she considers an unmitigated bore, but I learned to love it because Mrs. Lawrence takes us to the Music Center whenever the Metropolitan Opera is in town, and she also takes us to opera movies. One of them, *La Traviata*, was one of the most beautiful experiences I'd ever had.

In *La Traviata*, a woman gives up the man she loves because his father asks her to. I really thought she was foolish to do it. But anyway, he comes back just as she's dying of tuberculosis. I couldn't stop crying, it was so marvelously romantic. They didn't have penicillin then or any cure for tuberculosis. I wonder if they would have lived happily ever afterward if her disease had been cured.

I think his father was really mean to make her give him up. That kind of thing couldn't happen today. Or maybe it could. After all, she had been kind of a courtesan, which is still not exactly considered a great occupation.

Mrs. Lawrence was born in Russia, and there's a warm extravagance about her manner that always makes me feel good. Very often she sings her words to us instead of speaking them. It's kind of delightful. The atmosphere of Paula's house is very different from mine. They don't have a pool because Mrs. Lawrence says, "The water destroys my hair." Instead, they have wonderful gardens that she works in for hours a day when she isn't practicing. "I love being a housewife," she often sings. "Thank God I made enough money to retire. Thank God my records still do well. I have everything I need—my music, my beautiful daughter, my cooking, my flowers. I am a happy, happy woman."

Mrs. Lawrence divorced Paula's father somewhere in Europe, and it's as if he never existed. They don't even know where he is. Mrs. Lawrence has no desire to ever remarry. "Peace is wonderful," she sings.

My father died in an automobile accident when I was little, so I never knew him. But unlike Mrs. Lawrence, Sharon does want to remarry some day, and she's as busy at night with her dates as she is by day with the people who keep her looking beautiful. She's been popular with men since she was six. That's another point of embarrassment to me. I've never had a date in my whole sixteen years. Paula hasn't either, but it doesn't seem to bother her or Mrs. Lawrence.

I enjoy being at Paula's house much more than at my own, although, of course, I'd never hurt Sharon's feelings by saying so. The thing is, there's no tension there because Mrs. Lawrence accepts herself. If Sharon looked like that, she'd probably die. Mrs. Lawrence has dry, rusty, dyed hair that's tucked up in a messy bun, deep sagging wrinkles on her face, short unmanicured nails so she can play the piano, and she's as round and plain as a loaf of bakery pumpernickel. I don't find her extra weight unappealing. There's something motherly about it. Actually I never think of her that way because she has such a great personality.

When she saw us, she jumped up from the piano and held out her arms as if she hadn't seen us for months. "My angels," she sang. "Just in time. Marvelous hot borscht and pirogies." Mrs. Lawrence loves to cook and eat. She doesn't have a cook and does all her own cooking. "Why should I pay someone else to do what gives me so much pleasure?" she says. She's a big hugger and kisser. She threw her arms around each of us and plunked kisses on our cheeks.

"Hi, Mom," Paula said. "We're off to the Beverly Center. Can I have some money?"

"Certainly," she trilled. "But first you must taste."

She dragged us with her into the kitchen that smelled like happiness. I rarely go into the kitchen at my house because I always feel as if I'm intruding on the cook or the maid, but Mrs. Lawrence practically lives in her kitchen.

"When I was a child," she once told me, "we all slept in the kitchen for warmth."

We sat down at the table, and she gave us steaming bowls of hot cabbage soup with dollops of sour cream in the center, and pirogies. These are little Russian turnovers with meat inside.

"What is it, my little darling?" she trilled, noticing I wasn't attacking the food with my usual gusto.

Paula told her about the article. When she had finished, Mrs. Lawrence sang, "Americans are crazy. Eat, my little darlings, and let me tell you a few things."

I began to eat the wonderful soup, feeling it warm my discouraged heart, while she talked to us. "During World War II, when I was a child in Leningrad, every day people dropped dead in the streets of starvation. My father died and all of my brothers and sisters. We ate out of garbage pails. When there was nothing in the garbage pails, we caught and cooked rats."

"Rats!" Paula exclaimed. "How gross! You must be kidding, Mom."

"Rats," she repeated firmly. "All of the pets disappeared from the city. Our special Christmas meal was water and potato peelings. It taught me forever the value of food.

"Later on, when I was trying to get into La Scala, they told me to lose some weight. I starved myself. I went to the spas. I finally went to Switzerland for sleep therapy."

"What's that?" I asked, holding up my bowl for some more soup.

"They put you to sleep for two weeks so you can't eat."

"Two weeks. How absolutely awful. I mean, to be unconscious and not read the paper or watch television or smell the air."

"You are absolutely right, my little darling. After two weeks I had lost forty pounds, but—" her voice took on a tragic dimension "—I had also lost my voice."

"I didn't know that, Mom. You mean you couldn't sing well?"

"I couldn't sing at all. It took me six months to return to normal and after that I vowed never again. I needed my weight to support my voice.

"You know, they used to mock poor Lauritz Melchior and Kirsten Flagstad when they sang *Tristan and Isolde* because here were two fat people singing the most glorious love music in the world. People in the audience should have closed their eyes and been transported by their voices. I know a million thin people who can't sing."

"But that's the point," I said. "My mother is really worried about that newspaper story. She doesn't want to be embarrassed."

"Of course you know, Lois darling, that I would never criticize your mother. But you are not connected by an umbilical cord. Would you care if she put on weight?"

"Of course not. But that's different."

"Not as far as I can see. Why should anyone ever be embarrassed by a girl as lovely as you? You go on and on all the time about your weight, but I never hear you say anything good about yourself. Think of all your good qualities."

"Such as?"

"Such as your mind, for one. Such as your character, for two. I am proud that you're Paula's best friend."

"Nobody cares about those things. Only about the way you look."

"You look fine to me. Lovely hair and lovely skin and lovely smile. Nobody's perfect you know, my little darling."

"I suppose. But some people are more perfect than others."

"Enough of this useless gloom," Mrs. Lawrence said, reaching for her purse. "Go and enjoy yourself. Forget about this newspaper story. I am certain that such interference is unconstitutional. Just try to keep a little perspective. Being thin does not automatically make you happy. Focus on your good qualities."

Paula gave her a parting hug. "Unfortunately, Mom," she said, "boys don't care about anything but how you look."

Chapter Four

Mrs. Lawrence cheered us up a little, but as soon as we hit the Beverly Center I started to feel rotten again because we ran into a gang of in kids from school waiting in line with us to buy movie tickets. I never liked this particular group, but usually they left us alone.

One of them, Kevin, had a reputation for viciousness. "Hey, Lois," he asked with a sly grin, "did you see the story in this morning's paper?"

"Which story?" I asked, pretending innocence.

"About the war on flab. I read it this morning."

"Really?" Paula said. "When did you learn to read?"

Fortunately, just then, the line started to move. We had come to see a German movie called *Sugarbaby* that interested us because the ads asked, "Can a fat girl find love?"

I guess I should have known better than to expect it to be compassionate. It was about a really grotesque girl who works in a mortuary, overeats and has no friends. She has a lonely, boring life until she falls in love with a subway conductor who's kind of retarded, and she woos him with candy bars and good cooking. They begin an affair.

When his wife finds out, she follows them to a disco where they're dancing, knocks the girl down and starts to kick her. Instead of defending herself, the girl just rolls up into a ball on the ground and cries. The man is such a weak fink that he does nothing to protect her. His wife grabs his hand and drags him away, leaving the fat girl weeping on the floor.

The other people in the disco all stand around watching, but not one person goes to her aid, either during the attack or afterward. Nobody helps her up. Nobody comforts her, because she's supposed to be a joke. And the most ludicrous thing about the entire movie is that *she's* supposed to be the abnormal one. Not the thin, mean blond wife. Not the subway conductor to whom she's been so good. Not the people who stand around and let her be beaten. The fat girl was the nicest person in the film, but even so she was made to seem ridiculous.

At the end of the movie, apparently having recovered, she's down in the subway station again with her candy bars, approaching another subway conductor.

When the credits went on, Kevin's voice rang out, "Hey, Lois, maybe you should try that approach."

And another boy's voice answered, "She couldn't have me if she offered me a pound of Godiva chocolates."

"Did you hear the new ecology slogan?" Kevin called. "Save a whale, harpoon a fat chick."

I was so upset that I was about to run away with Paula, but then I got angry. "Listen, you nerds," I said, turning to them defiantly when the lights went on. "I'd rather be fat than be a jerk or a stoner. I'd rather be healthy and fat than be anorexic or run into the bathroom between classes to throw up like the bulimics. You all remind me of that play we read in drama, called *Rhinoceros*. Anybody who doesn't look like a rhinoceros is made to feel ugly."

"I'd rather be a rhinoceros than an elephant," said Dory, one of the girls I knew for a fact was bulimic.

"Don't get mad, Lois," called Kevin. "Where's your sense of humor?"

"I left it where you left your brains."

"Come on, you kids," said an usher. "Break it up. Move!"

Paula and I left with as much dignity as we could muster, but we were both pretty upset by the encounter. We shopped for a few minutes to cheer us up. Paula has two favorite slogans about shopping. "Shop till you drop" and "When the going gets tough, the tough go shopping." They always make us laugh. She said them now, but neither one of us laughed.

Our hearts weren't really in shopping, so we went to the Hard Rock Café downstairs for dinner. Wouldn't you know? The same kids from the movie were waiting in line. "Just watch this," I told Paula, my sense of humor partially restored. "We're going to get a little of our own back."

I pulled out Sharon's Gold Card that the Hard Rock gives celebrities to let them in without waiting. Waving it at our tormentors, we went down to the front of the line.

"Aw. Come on, Paula. Come on, Lois. Take us in with you. We were only kidding around," Kevin called.

"Get stuffed," Paula called back.

"Go harpoon a chick," I added as we swept regally into the restaurant.

Chapter Five

When I got home that night, I found that Sharon and Missy had already made plans for the war on flab.

"Look," Sharon said, stepping on a tremendous, high-tech stainless-steel scale. "The newest in scales. I'll show you how it works. My ideal weight is a hundred and ten. Therefore, I'll adjust it to a hundred and ten. Now watch what happens."

She stepped on the scale, and a robot voice rumbled up from it. "Uh-oh," the voice said. "You are two pounds over your ideal weight. You will have to try a little harder."

"I'm sorry," Sharon said in a crestfallen voice. "I'll have it off by tomorrow."

"Mom. I don't believe it. Are you apologizing to a scale?"

Sheepishly she hopped off. "Isn't that silly?"

"What does it do if your weight is just right?"

"Let's see."

She put it on a hundred and twelve, and when she stepped on, the voice rumbled, "Very, very good. You are right on target. Keep up the good work."

"You want to try it, Lois?"

"Not on your life."

She lit a cigarette and paced back and forth. "I can't believe that I've put on two pounds. Tomorrow, total fast."

"Oh, Mom. You weigh less at forty than I weighed at ten."

"Shussh! Thirty-three, not forty!"

Sharon's appearance affects her career, so her face and figure have been obsessions in my home for as long as I can remember. She tells the press that she had me at seventeen.

"This is what I found for you," Missy said, holding up a picture from *Life*. "I'll put it up with magnets on one of the refrigerators."

I looked at the picture. It was a starving Ethiopian, a skeletal boy from central Tigris who had walked for more than fifty days to the Sudan. His parents had died on the march, and you could see every bone in his body. He looked like those people in concentration camps.

"That's a very sad picture, Missy, but I don't get your point."

"This is to remind you that it's disgusting to be a glutton while so many other people are starving."

"That picture would have exactly the opposite effect on me. Ethiopians don't want to starve. Nobody wants to starve. So why should I starve voluntarily? It certainly won't help *them*."

"I was only trying to help you." She sniffed indignantly. I've never known anybody as thin-skinned as

Missy. That's an interesting word, isn't it? Thin-skinned means you're too sensitive. Thin isn't a complimentary word used that way.

"And now for the big surprise," Sharon said with such enthusiasm you'd have thought she was planning a party. "We've made an appointment for you with a hypnotist."

"You've got to be kidding. I don't want to be hypnotized."

"Darling, you'll love it. I know lots of people who've gone to hypnotists to stop smoking and eating. It's the easiest way out of your dilemma."

"I don't know," I said suspiciously. "How does it work?"

"He just puts you under and gives you a posthypnotic suggestion not to eat."

"And everyone says Dr. Danto's the best hypnotist in L.A.," Missy added. She held out a copy of *L.A. Magazine* to me. "Here's his ad. It's the biggest of any hypnotist."

The Danto Method of Hypnosis Specialists In
Weight Control
Smoking Cessation
Self-hypnosis
Achieving Relaxation
Overcoming Insomnia
Overcoming Fears
Reducing Stress
Controlling Addictions
Self-Confidence
Success Attitudes
Relief of Pain
Sales Motivation

Overcoming Anxieties
Improving Study Habits

"Missy has already made an appointment for you,"
Sharon said.

"Thanks a lot. Don't you at least think I should be
consulted?"

"Ungrateful as usual," Missy said. "I had to call at
once so he could fit you in. Your mother spoke to him
herself. Otherwise, you would have had to wait three
months for an appointment."

I looked again at the list of his specialties. "Mom, it
all looks like a fake to me. If it were that easy to achieve
self-confidence, everybody in L.A. would be seeing
him."

"Everybody is," Missy said. "I just told you that."

"Would either of you care to tell me what it costs?"

A look of concern crossed Missy's face. "A hundred
and fifty dollars for the first visit and fifty dollars a visit
each time afterward. So try to make it count. It's not
covered by health insurance, and as I told you this
morning, Sharon hasn't worked in eight months."

"Are we going to run out of money, Mom?"

"Of course not. We just have to pull in a little until I
get a job. Marty's working on several right now. I am
letting the chauffeur go."

"Oh, Mom. I'm sorry. Is it because of the hypnotist?"

"Of course not, darling. He made almost as much as
that a week. It just seemed wasteful to keep him on.
Everybody comes to the house, and actually, I like to
drive myself."

"Nevertheless," Missy said, "this is an unplanned-
for expense, Lois, so try to make it work. Actually, if

you were my kid, I'd take away your credit cards and send you out to work. All you need is a job and a little discipline. I've worked hard since I was six. Nobody ever gave me your advantages.''

"So what does that have to do with me? I'm sorry you had a lousy childhood, Missy, but to tell you the truth, I'm sick of hearing about it."

Her face turned red. "If you were my kid, Lois, I'd kill you for being so rude."

"You wouldn't have to," I snapped, equally fed up with her. "If I were your kid, I'd have committed suicide long ago."

"We do not appreciate your smart remarks." She always uses the pronoun *we* as if she and Sharon are one person. Really, she's like a middle-aged groupie. Whenever I complain about her, Sharon says she couldn't do without her and she reminds me about Missy's poor, deprived childhood. Missy will probably trade on that until she's in an old-age home. If she weren't such an opinionated pill, maybe I could be more sympathetic.

"Once and for all, Mom," I said, "will you tell Missy to get off my back? I don't need two mothers."

Sharon didn't answer.

"Mom. Do you hear me?"

"I'm not exactly listening. I'm too upset."

"About my weight?"

"No. About mine. I'll never understand how I put on those two pounds. Maybe it's just water. Missy, call the doctor tomorrow and have him send over a diuretic. And tell Flash that I need an extra hour."

I hurried to my room to phone Paula. "Oooh," she said when I told her about the hypnotist, "spooky."

"He calls himself Dr. Danto. Did you ever hear of a medical degree in hypnosis?" I asked her.

"Of course not! He probably also sells snake oil for warts. I understand they can't hypnotize you if you resist."

"I wouldn't dare to resist at those prices. Missy has threatened to kill me."

Paula giggled. "You know she really loves you. She just has a very funny way of showing it. Drive over here the minute you get through and try to remember every detail. Maybe he'll be young and handsome. Or maybe he'll be an evil manipulator who wants to get you in his power and ravish you. Listen, ask him if he can hypnotize me to be smarter in math."

"He's a hypnotist! Not a magician!"

"Very, very funny!"

"Well," we said together in one of our standard routines. "As the undertaker said, 'Remains to be seen.'"

Dr. Danto's office was in an ordinary high rise on San Vicente in Brentwood. I took the elevator to the fifth floor, timidly opened the heavy mahogany door and peeped in. Nothing glamorous or spooky. No scent of incense. No crystal ball.

I had expected something like the Haunted House at Disneyland, but this office was filled with leather furniture and had classy magazines. The walls were covered with swirling finger-paint paintings in pink and gray and black, the year's most trendy colors in L.A. Actually, this office was a carbon copy of my dentist's office. They must have used the same decorator. I was a little disappointed by the lack of mystery.

The nurse who came out to greet me was dressed in Reeboks, white jeans and a chic white bat-wing blouse. She wore a gold Rolex, half a dozen gold chains and large gold hoop earrings beneath a short blond frosted hairdo. She was probably about fifty but had a great body and an unlined, sunburned face. "Hi, Lois," she said warmly. "I'm Helen."

I filled out a form, handed her a check, then settled back for a delicious interlude with an article from *Gourmet*, "Five Favorite Desserts from Soufflé to Sorbet." I studied the picture of the Rich Lemon Mousse, made with fresh lemon juice and heavy cream and decorated with sprigs of fresh mint, and decided to pick up the ingredients when I got through and make it with Paula at her house. My mouth watered in anticipation. I was almost sorry when the doctor opened his office door, smiled warmly and said, "Hi, there," and beckoned me in.

Dr. Danto was about forty, but as trendy, attractive and sunburned as his nurse, with thick gray hair, penetrating blue eyes and a warm, pleasant expression on his face. He was dressed in cowboy boots, suede slacks and a beige hand-knit Irish fisherman sweater. The walls of his inner office were covered with pictures of him with various celebrities as well as framed mementos of his having run in several marathons. I hoped he wasn't going to suggest that for me.

"You must be Lois." He smiled, as if my arrival were the greatest thing that had happened to him that day. It was hard not to like him.

"Call me Arthur," he said, motioning me to a soft pink velvet armchair. Then, for the next hour, we interviewed each other. He was nice about it. Probably one of the courses he'd taken at Hypnotists' School was "How to Put Wary Patients at Ease."

"How did you get into this line of work?" I asked.

"I used to be a police officer, and I learned to do hypnosis in connection with my police work."

"Did you make people admit they'd done terrible crimes? Like the Hillside Strangler?"

"No. You can't make people under hypnosis reveal what they wouldn't otherwise tell you or do what they don't want to do. As a matter of fact, the Hillside Strangler managed to fool his hypnotist."

"Then how did you use it when you were a policeman?" I was really interested, and I was glad he didn't treat me like a pesky kid.

"Oh, in a variety of ways. For example, one client had forgotten the combination for his safe, but he easily recalled it under hypnosis. A colleague of mine was cleaning his gun when the doorbell rang. He put it somewhere to keep it out of harm's way and then couldn't remember where. Naturally, he was pretty upset because he had young children around. It took only one session for him to recall that he'd put it in a gap in the wall underneath the stairs. I also help patients with a variety of problems. People who bite and pick at their nails, people with phobias, alcoholics, gamblers, drug addicts, coffee addicts, anorexics, bulimics and food addicts."

"Does it depress you?"

"No. I feel good about trying to help."

"Can you help everybody?"

"Not those who don't want to be helped. Not those who won't help themselves. After all, hypnosis is suggestion, not thought control."

"Can you help me?"

"I hope so."

"Can everybody be hypnotized?"

"Not people who aren't very bright."

"Can I be hypnotized?"

"Definitely. You're a very smart girl. I'm sure you do very well in school. Am I right?"

"Yes. I'm a straight-A student, but nobody seems to care about that very much."

"Now tell me exactly why you want to be hypnotized."

"I'd like to get thin, of course. I don't like to stand out this way. Everybody would get off my back then and not object when I wear bright colors. Now, whenever I do, my mother and her secretary try to talk me out of them because they say they accentuate my fat. They want me to wear dark colors all the time, as if I'm in mourning for my figure." He sat quietly, waiting for me to continue.

"When you're fat," I went on, "you kind of lose your privacy. Even strangers think they can comment about you, as if being fat makes you hard of hearing. Once a lady said to her little girl, right in front of me, 'If you eat any more of that candy you'll look like *her* when you grow up.' Isn't that unbelievably tactless? So, of course, I want to do it for myself, but even more for my mother. She thinks it's a disgrace for a beautiful actress to have a blimp for a daughter. She's embarrassed at being seen with me. But I've never been able to get thin on my own. The truth of the matter is that I don't want to stop eating. I love to eat. It's my favorite hobby."

"I like to eat, too," he answered. "Everybody likes to eat. But we *can* change your eating habits. We can train you to eat the right foods so that little by little, almost imperceptibly, you will lose two pounds a week for twenty weeks. What do you say about that?"

"Great, if it's that easy! I'm real curious anyhow about what it feels like to be hypnotized. How will I know? Will I be unconscious?"

"Certainly not. You will be conscious of everything. You will hear that clock chime. You may start to feel cold as your circulation slows down. You may feel a heaviness pressing against your arms and legs. But you will feel good. And remember that I cannot make you do anything you do not want to do."

Nobody else ever could either, I thought. That's one of the things Missy always complains about.

Chapter Six

He told me to lie back on the lounge and to focus my eyes on a special lamp across the room, which had wavy blue liquid heaving back and forth like the waves of an ocean. Then he began to talk to me, and his voice was reassuring and absolutely wonderful, low and soothing.

He told me a story. I was at the beach. I could feel the warm sand under my toes and smell the brine and see and hear the waves breaking on the shore. Above my head sea gulls were screeching. I was walking along the sand, picking up seashells, feeling happy, light and free. The sun was shining on my face, and the balmy breeze played with my hair.

"You're not thinking about food," he said, but he wasn't quite correct. From somewhere on the imaginary beach came the delicious fragrance of an outdoor barbecue.

Then he told me that when I awakened I would feel very good and that before going to sleep at night I would put my hands on my stomach and repeat, over and over again, "I control food. Food does not control me. I will eat sensibly and sparingly. I will not eat fattening foods. I will not eat between meals."

Then he told me to wake up.

"Was I hypnotized?"

"Yes, indeed."

"How do you know? I'm not sure I was."

"How long do you think you were under?"

"Ten minutes?"

"Look at the clock!"

"Wow! Half an hour! But I was aware of everything."

"You always will be. I promised you that. But you'll be able to go into an even deeper trance next time."

I felt so hopeful after leaving him that I decided not to get the ingredients for the lemon mousse after all. I drove quickly to Paula's house.

"Lois has just been to a hypnotist to stop eating," Paula announced to her mother, who was sitting at the piano.

Mrs. Lawrence broke into song. "La-la-la, American nonsense," she sang up and down the scale. "American nonsense, la-la-la."

"I'm dying to see if the posthypnotic suggestion works," I told Paula. "Quickly. Before it wears off."

We left Mrs. Lawrence to her practicing and went to the family room, where Paula has her own soda fountain for entertaining. She took a quart of Häagen-Dazs Chocolate Chocolate Chip out of the freezer, filled two bowls with it, spooned on fudge sauce and chocolate sprinkles and topped it all off with real whipped cream and a maraschino cherry. Pig heaven!

"Now theoretically," Paula said with her mouth full, "you shouldn't want this. You should feel like an alcoholic on antidrink medication. Super-strong aversion!"

I sat there looking at the sundae, waiting for the posthypnotic suggestions to take over, but no mysterious voice welled up inside me to help me refrain.

"No aversion," I said. "Let's see what happens if I just taste it. Maybe it will start then."

I picked up my spoon and tasted the sundae. When next I came up for air, my dish was empty.

"It certainly isn't working yet," Paula said.

"Thanks a lot for telling me." I really felt awful. In fact, I could not recall a moment in a lifetime of feeling bad about being fat when I felt as completely awful as just then. I hated to disappoint Dr. Danto.

Paula was always aware of my feelings. "Don't be upset. Maybe it will start to work tomorrow."

"Maybe. He gave me an exercise to do."

As soon as I got into bed that night, I began the exercise he had shown me. I only got as far as saying it three times before I fell asleep. I awakened the next morning as hungry as usual but anxious to see if maybe by now I'd be able to change my eating habits.

I started with half a grapefruit and sugar substitute. So far so good! Then I tried to eat bran cereal and skimmed milk. The bran tasted like shredded cardboard and the milk reminded me of the chalky milk of magnesia one of my childhood nannies used to force on me. I sat there looking at the food with revulsion. What point is there in eating at all if everything tastes awful?

I finally dumped it all down the disposal and tore into two raisin bagels slathered with thick cream cheese.

Just then Paula called. "Did it work?"

"No! I just had a big breakfast and I hate myself."

"Are we going shopping today?"

"I don't know. Maybe after lunch. I'd better stay here alone and try to diet. I'm going to pretend I'm in jail and they're only feeding me bread and water."

"What kind of bread?"

"Raisin pumpernickel, natch."

I went back to sleep and set my alarm for noon in order to avoid temptation. I kept doing Dr. Danto's exercises until I fell asleep again. When I awakened, I was ravenous. But I tried. I really did. But cottage cheese did not taste the same as cream cheese, yogurt did not taste like gelato, and Cool Whip was not a substitute for thick whipped cream. I was so miserable eating those awful foods that I gave up and phoned Paula.

"Hey, Paula! Want to go to the Beverly Center with a hypnosis failure?"

"Pick you up in ten minutes. Don't be discouraged. I found an article that will interest you. It's not your fault."

The article was about fifty college students who responded to an ad that said, "Lose weight by watching television."

During the next few weeks, the students watched a hypnotic weight-loss video over and over. Half saw a version without subliminal stimulation and the other half watched a weight-loss video containing subliminal phrases they weren't aware of, such as, "Don't eat" and "Hang in there."

At the end of the experiment, there was no weight-loss difference between the two groups. The average weight loss for both groups was about a pound.

"See," Paula said, trying to comfort me. "Maybe the method's just no good. It's not your fault. You're not a hypnosis failure. It looks to me as if hypnosis is the failure. Are you going to tell Dr. Danto about this method?"

"No. I couldn't bear to hurt his feelings."

Chapter Seven

At my next session, Dr. Danto asked, "Would you like to get on the scale?"

"No, thank you. I wouldn't like it at all. I don't know if I've put on any weight, but I'm certain I haven't lost any either."

"What makes you think that? Have you weighed yourself?"

"No. I never do. The scale is my enemy. But I can tell from the way my clothes fit. I used your techniques, but they didn't seem to work. Since visiting you, I've been thinking about food even more than before."

Then he began to ask me a series of questions such as: Did I feel inferior to Sharon? Did I feel a need to compete for attention? Did I eat because I missed a father? That kind of thing.

"I don't feel inferior to my mother," I said indignantly. "I never even think about things that way. And

I don't want to compete for attention. I don't want people to look at me. I want them *not* to look at me. I couldn't be as brave as she is in a million years. Always having to smile and look perky. Being in the movies is the world's worst job. As for my father, he died in an automobile accident when I was a baby, so I never knew him at all. My mom tells me she adored him, but she's not morbid about it. I think she'd like to marry again, but she just hasn't found a significant other. I don't eat because I miss a father. I eat because I like to. Unfortunately, it makes me fat."

"May I ask you a very personal question, Lois?"

"What were all the other questions? Weren't they personal?"

"Do you have a boyfriend?"

"No."

"Do you think you might be eating as a substitute for love, or—" he cleared his throat "—sex?"

"I don't feel unloved. Sharon loves me. My friend Paula loves me."

"But if you had a boyfriend who loved you, wouldn't that change things somewhat?"

"It sure would. We could try out lots of new restaurants together. And I'd cook for him. I'm always looking for someone to try new recipes out on. Maybe we'd even cook together. I'd love that."

Dr. Danto emitted an almost imperceptible sigh. "Well, let's see what we can do this time."

He put me under again, and I found myself really enjoying the experience. Hypnosis is great! I wonder if while he's curing people of their other addictions he ever makes them into hypnosis freaks. Know what it feels like? It feels like that great gas the dentist sometimes uses. You're conscious but happy and floating and everything seems really wonderful. When you wake up, you feel as if you've been away on vacation.

When he awakened me he gave me the same instructions again for hypnotizing myself before falling asleep. "This week the posthypnotic suggestions should work a little better," he assured me. "But it will probably take six sessions for your complete reeducation."

At my next hypnosis visit, I found that I had put on five more pounds. By the end of the sixth, I'd put on another two. The problem was that every time I thought of eating sensibly and sparingly I became ravenously hungry.

"That's it," Sharon said. "Tell him you won't be seeing him any longer."

To my amazement, I ended up comforting him. "It's not your fault," I assured him. Then I told him about the college study. He hadn't known about it, and he was grateful to me for bringing it to his attention.

Paula had dropped me off and gone to get Juliet nails. She was waiting outside, and she waved her nails at me. "Aren't they gorgeous?" she crowed. "The manicurist had two long pinky nails of pure gold. Where do you want to go?"

"Let's go to Will Rogers Park. I feel like walking."

She drove with her hands splayed out on the wheel, so intent on protecting her nails that she passed a red light.

"Oh, God," I moaned as a cop's siren went off behind us. "I think you did it."

He got out of his car and walked over to us. "In a hurry, girls?"

"Not really," Paula said.

"License and registration."

"Would you mind waiting about fifteen minutes?"

"What?" His face registered shock.

"My nails are still wet and this manicure cost a fortune."

He looked at her in disbelief, then began to howl with laughter. After he had calmed down, he said, "That's the best I've heard all day. What's your name?"

"Paula Lawrence."

"And where are you going?"

"Will Rogers State Park."

"Think you could drive there at normal speed?"

"I think so." Her fingers were still splayed on the steering wheel.

He looked down at her nails and began to laugh again. "I really needed this. I don't laugh enough on my job. Did you know that people can cure themselves of diseases if they laugh enough?"

Paula rolled her eyes at me.

"All right, Paula. I'll let you off this time, but I'd better never stop you again. Is that clear?"

"It's clear. It's clear. I promise. I'll never, never run a red light again."

As soon as he was out of sight, we got so hysterical that we laughed all the way to the park.

We parked the car and walked up one of the bridle paths to a high point where there's a bench and you can look out all over the city. The sun was pleasant and warm and comforting, and the lovely smell of eucalyptus surrounded us. Little by little I started to feel less bad about the hypnosis.

"What do you think Sharon will do now?" Paula asked.

"Who knows? I wish they'd let me alone," I said, sighing. "I hate all the language of reducing. Go for the burn. Battle of the bulge. War against flab."

"I feel the same way. So let's forget about it and enjoy the day. Wasn't that policeman funny?"

We began to laugh again.

After a while we walked down to the ring to watch the riding lessons. I admired the riders, the graceful bodies of the horses, their sleek muscles rippling as they went over the jumps. I think riders have to have a lot of courage for that. It seemed to me that the riders were very lucky that they had bodies they could use so skillfully, instead of bodies that were burdens to them.

Chapter Eight

That night, Sharon, Missy and I conferred on the next battle of the war.

"Pay her for each pound she loses," Missy advised, "and give her no other money. We should have also paid that quack hypnotist after the results. He would have had a little more incentive. Well, the hypnosis failed, but there are other methods that seem to be getting results."

Then she proceeded to describe them. One was to wire the mouth shut and leave room only for a straw so that the patient is reduced to a liquid diet, and not much of that either. Yeccch! Another was a bypass operation that surgically staples off a portion of the stomach so that it can hold only small amounts of food. Double yeccch! A third was called the Gastric Bubble. It's a soft polyurethene sac that's deflated and inserted into the stomach with a plastic tube. Then it's inflated and floats around in the stomach and helps to satisfy the feelings of hunger. After four months it's deflated and removed.

According to Missy, one woman lost eighty-three pounds with it. "This bubble method is the answer," she said. "It makes people feel wonderful."

"Get real," I said. "I would never consent to such physical mutilation."

"Being fat is physical mutilation," Missy answered.

"I know what we should do now." Sharon clapped her hands with sudden inspiration. "We'll send her to a psychiatrist."

"I am not going to a shrink. I'm perfectly fine mentally."

"No you're not. If you were, you wouldn't still be fat. Missy, make an appointment for her with Dr. Crouch."

"Oh, God! Not him!"

I'd been hearing about him for a long time. Sharon had some friends who had Dr. Crouch on the payroll like a family retainer. Every member of that family had been going to him for years. Sometimes alone, sometimes in small groups, sometimes in one large quarreling ball. They even once got into a fistfight in front of him.

They never made a move without consulting him, just the way ancient Greeks used to consult soothsayers. They took him along on every family vacation, and he sat at the head table at weddings. Nobody ever made a decision without consulting him, and the minute someone married into that family, they also started to see him.

"How do you know he's competent to help me, Mom?"

"Would they have used him for years if he weren't competent?"

"If he's really competent, how come they have to keep seeing him for so many years?"

"That's the point. They want to keep seeing him."

"I don't want to go."

"Please go, just once at least. Do it for me! So I feel I'm trying everything possible to help you."

"All right. I'll go once. But don't expect any miracles. Each time you're disappointed in me, Mom, it really upsets me."

"Is that really what upsets you, or are you afraid?"

"Of course I'm not afraid. Why should I be afraid of finding out that I'm mentally unbalanced?"

"Do you think you are?" Now Sharon was getting upset. Being fat was one thing. Being fat plus being nuts was even worse.

"I was joking, Mom. I definitely don't think being fat is like being mentally sick. It's a waste of money."

"But he'll try to help you," Missy said. "So at least go with an open mind." I didn't. I went in with a closed mind, and I left with it even more tightly closed. He couldn't have opened my mind with a can opener. To begin with, he had my least favorite hairdo: the hair parted directly above the ear so that extra long side hair can be pulled across the bald top. It looks ridiculous. I've never really understood why some men do this. Who do they think they're fooling? It's better to be attractively bald like Yul Brynner or Robert Duvall than to try to pretend you're not bald. There's something dishonest about it that I don't like.

Although he had no hair on top, he had Astroturf growing out of his nostrils, and he gnawed on his cuticles right through my visit. Occasionally he began to clean his ear with the end of his pen. Gross! What a joke that this weird creep was supposed to cure me of being fat. I looked better than he did. I bet creepy people like that become shrinks because if they didn't nobody would listen to them. This way, they're always in the position of being right. "Tell me about your problem," he began, and so I started to talk just to avoid boredom.

"I'm not as concerned about my weight as Sharon is. I don't think the first commandment is, 'Thou shalt not be fat.'"

"I don't think it's a commandment at all."

Oh, God! No sense of humor.

"Half of me wants to get thin," I continued, "but the other half of me resents the fact that nobody regards you as a human being unless you do."

"Aha! What else do you resent?"

"I resent the way everyone makes fun of fat people."

He pounced as if he'd suddenly found a gold nugget. "What do you mean by 'everyone'?"

"That's just what I mean. Fat people are fair game. It's always hunting season."

"Do you have feelings of persecution?"

"Not feelings! Actual experiences! And it's not fair. I've read all about it, and most of the problem is genetic. You inherit a certain body type. An endomorphic body type is heavy and rounded and a mesomorphic body type is husky and muscular. Tough luck if you're born either an endo or a meso. Chances are you're going to be overweight. So if so much is genetic, why should people torture themselves trying to achieve an impossible ideal? Why should everybody have to conform to one model?"

"You resent the necessity to conform?"

"I sure do."

He wrote that down, looked at his watch and said, "Our time is just about up. Let me ask you a question."

"Okay. Go ahead."

"Why do you call your mother by her first name?"

"You mean I should call her Mrs. Long?"

"Of course not. Why don't you call her Mom?"

"I do. I call her Mom, Mother, Sharon and Hey, You."

"Do you call her Sharon because you don't feel close to her?"

"No. I call her Sharon because I don't feel close to you."

He looked at his watch. "We'll continue with this next time."

"The guy's a real jerk," I told Sharon that night, "and I'm never going back."

"Should we find another therapist?"

"Absolutely not. I don't need or want a shrink."

Chapter Nine

Sharon's next idea was that we should go to a fat farm together. She selected one called Sunnyasi that was based on the idea of total austerity. A very serious place! "Everyone says it's fatproof," she said, "and I wouldn't mind taking off a few pounds myself."

"But that place is twenty-five hundred a week per person," Missy objected. "I thought you were going to begin economizing."

For once I was on Missy's side. "I totally agree. We should economize. Besides, I've heard about that place in school. Some of the kids' mothers have been there. It's like marine boot camp. All of the guests have to share the same two bathrooms and they only feed you air. They put a cowbell on the refrigerator to guard it against desperate raiders. If you're caught raiding, everybody stands around you in a circle crying, 'Shame! Shame!' They should pay us to go to a place like that."

"Stop exaggerating. You don't know anything about it. Make a reservation for us, Missy, for the day Lois finishes school."

"All right. I'll go if I have to, but I'm going to hate it."

"You hate everything except eating," Missy said.

Ignoring her, I rushed to phone Paula with my terrible news. "I can't picture Sharon getting any thinner," she said.

"What can I tell you? It's an obsession! I dread the thought of being there. Even more than going to that moldy shrink."

"Well, maybe it won't be too bad," she said, trying to cheer me up. "All the celebrities go! And maybe you'll meet a nice guy. Remember that you're going to Yosemite with my mom and me. Going to Sunnyasi will get you in shape for hiking."

"The problem is, what will get me in shape for Sunnyasi?"

"Hey, Lois, I just heard there's a spa for overweight pets."

"You're kidding!"

"No! Honest! They put pets on four low-filler, high-protein snacks a day and take them for brisk walks. Their motto is, 'A fat dog is an unhappy dog.'"

Can you imagine? Even pets! Wherever I turned during the next few weeks, the conversation was about fat.

We left on June 20, as soon as school was out, and it was every bit as bad as I'd heard. You wouldn't believe the nerve and pretentiousness of the place. It accepted only six to eight guests each week and put them on a Spartan diet of fruit juices, yogurt, raw vegetables, seeds, sprouts, nuts and herbal teas. Can you imagine charging twenty-five hundred a person for seeds?

It was run by a woman who acted like the ex-commandant of a concentration camp. Her name was Sonja, a Swedish lady with a magnificent thick blond braid down to her waist. She was probably about fifty but had a sculpted body that would have been a work of art for any age.

She welcomed us with a steely smile and then her assistant, Ingrid, another magnificent intimidating body, came into the room wearing a Lycra leotard cut so high on the hips that it was practically under her arms. She genuflected before Sharon, cast a disapproving glance at me and then escorted us to our cell. I was already feeling depressed, inferior and stubborn, and her dismayed look didn't improve my mood. Did she think we were shelling out twenty-five hundred a week for her to sneer at me? She reminded me of certain salespeople on Rodeo Drive who won't even wait on you unless you're dressed up. Mrs. Lawrence always complained about it indignantly. "Never in my entire life," she said, "will I dress up to impress salespeople."

This Ingrid also reminded me of certain teachers in school who scold you for not knowing something instead of teaching you what you don't know. They act offended if you're not smart to begin with. I was there to get thin, and she was annoyed that I was fat.

As soon as she had gone, I turned to Sharon in shock. "Mom, we're in the hands of con artists. This is a super dump. It reminds me of the motel in *Psycho*. We had nicer rooms than this at summer camp. They should pay us to be here. These are the narrowest beds I've ever seen. It's like the story of Procrustes."

"Who's Procrustes? What movie?"

"It's not a movie and it's not a Greek restaurant. Procrustes was a legendary robber in Greek mythology who made everybody fit on the same bed. If they were too tall, he'd lop off their legs, and if they were too short, he'd stretch them."

"What a silly thing to do. Why would he do that if he was a robber?"

"I don't know. People did lots of strange things in myths. Like making love to a swan. The point I'm trying to make is that we're all supposed to automatically fit these narrow pallets."

"Stop being so critical, Lois. You'll never get thin if you keep a closed mind. They don't want the rooms to be too comfortable. That's why there are no TVs. They want us out exercising, not spending time in the rooms."

"I'll die without a TV."

"Give it a chance. You might enjoy the change."

Her friends had warned her about what to expect, so she was being a good sport about "roughing it," as if she were playing a role in a film, kind of like Goldie Hawn in *Private Benjamin*.

Besides, Sharon is accustomed to suffering for her career. It wasn't hard for her to look sensational when she was a girl, but she really has to work at it now. It's hard, expensive work. A lot of sweating and straining and spending money and saying no to wonderful food.

The terrible irony about all of this is that since she turned forty, as Missy keeps reminding us, even with all of her work and worrying she isn't getting important parts any longer. It's not personal! It's the nature of the industry. Some of her friends haven't worked in years. But even so, they go on exercising and starving themselves so that if by some miracle a wonderful role comes their way, they'll be ready.

Sharon and her friends don't only torture themselves by exercising and not eating. They're constantly remaking their bodies. They've had tummy tucks, chin tucks, neck tucks, buttocks-lifts, face-lifts, breast-lifts and fat sucked out of their thighs. They've had metal whisks dermabrade their faces, varicose veins stripped, eyelash transplants and eyeliner tattooed around their eyes so they don't have to worry about not having makeup on when they're sleeping or swimming.

They've all had their teeth ground down and capped with gleaming porcelain fakes, and they regularly have the hair around their mouths, eyebrows, legs and thighs pulled off with hot wax.

Sharon once had her face chemically peeled, and she was in such excruciating agony that no amount of painkillers could help for several days. "Peeled" doesn't really explain how awful the procedure is. It isn't nice and simple and pleasant like peeling a banana. It's a euphemism! What really happens is that the old skin is burned off and this causes the very same kind of terrible pain that goes with a real burn.

The peeling did what it was supposed to do, of course. It got rid of all the little lines that her two facelifts couldn't erase, lines that most people would never even notice but that the camera certainly did. The peeling was the only time I ever heard her complain about something she had to do for her career.

"This is one thing," she vowed, "that I would absolutely never go through again. Not even if it meant the end of my career."

It was the one time she couldn't say, "Beauty knows no pain."

Chapter Ten

We met the other unfortunate victims at "dinner" that night. There were eight people altogether, and all of them were a lot thinner than I. Six women, including me, and two men. Sharon knew two of the women from "the industry."

One of the men was married to one of the women. "We spend our vacation here every year," the wife said.

Can you imagine spending a vacation denying yourself food? I can just hear them reporting to their friends.

"So what did you do on your vacation?"

"I starved myself. I never had as much fun in my entire life."

The other man, Eric Stradletter, was an absolute doll; a sweet, kind man who owned one of L.A.'s hottest nouvelle cuisine restaurants, The Elegant Panther. He was about fifty but still good-looking, with a leathery suntanned face, merry blue eyes and a shock of white hair, kind of on the order of James Coburn.

He had come to take off some weight before going to France to make his annual tour of the great restaurants. Apart from a little potbelly, he didn't look the slightest bit fat to me. I could see that he was immediately taken with Sharon.

He talked to us right through a starvation dinner of miso soup and seaweed crackers, amusing us with food stories. For example, Chinese and other Southeast Asian peoples do not like milk. That's why there are no milk dishes in Chinese menus.

"But they serve ice cream for dessert," I pointed out.

"The concession to American tastes."

He also told us that Asian people eat things such as honey ants, locusts, grubs, giant water bugs, roaches, beetles and crickets. They boil them, soak them in vinegar and consider them delicacies.

"Are they fattening?" I asked to be funny.

"Maybe the giant water bugs, but probably not the others," he joked back. I liked him.

He also explained that nouvelle cuisine, the food he served in his restaurant, didn't just mean tiny little portions. It meant light on the sauces, heavy on fresh fruits and vegetables, and experimentation with marvelous new combinations of foods such as goat cheese and shitake mushrooms.

Sharon and I talked about him that night before falling asleep.

"Ingrid said he's been recently widowed," she said.

"I like him, Mom. Do you?"

"Kind of. We'll see what develops. After tonight's dinner, I don't have enough energy to really like anybody but you."

We began to giggle the way Paula and I always do. "Mom. These are the hardest beds I've ever slept in."

"Think how good it will feel when we go home."

I reached over and took her hand, and we fell asleep holding hands that way. In my entire sixteen years this was the first time we'd slept in the same room.

The next day we stopped giggling.

This was the routine at Sunnyasi. Up at six in the morning for a breakfast of orange juice. A two-hour hike, calisthenics in the pool and an early lunch of tiny rounds of some kind of white fish and about a quarter cup of julienned zucchini and carrots. Dessert was a quarter glass of apple juice.

After lunch there was weight lifting, aerobics, pool exercise, yoga and a massage. My body was so sore that the massage felt wonderful, but I felt kind of sorry for the poor masseuse who had to work so hard with my fat body. I kept falling asleep during the massage to delicious dreams of wheat cakes dripping with butter and maple syrup and ringed with sausages.

That evening we had another marvelous dinner of miso soup and seaweed crackers with a few bean sprouts. Sharon and Eric went walking after dinner, and I hurried to bed. Although absolutely exhausted, I was too hungry to sleep, and besides, I was physically uncomfortable. My heels were blistered, my shinsplints hurt and my thighs were red and inflamed from the chafing of my shorts.

I was trying to forget my sorrows in a book when Sharon came in. Her face was flushed and happy.

"So! What do you think of him, Mom?"

"He's a really fine man, and you know what else? He's seen every one of my films."

"How does he like this gulag?"

"He likes it very much. He's been here several times before, and he says that by the end of the week it seems easier. Think positively, Lois. We're getting rid of all the impurities in our bodies."

"We're also starving to death. What a rip-off. I bet prisoners at San Quentin are fed more than this. I'm getting ready to break out. If you want to come with me, start knotting your sheets and pillowcases together."

Sharon didn't answer. She was asleep.

The routine was the same the next day, but the morning hike was a lot harder. Half of it was uphill. "Keep up. Keep up," Ingrid kept calling to me. I was completely miserable and knew there was no way I could get through an even longer hike the next day.

When we set out the next morning, I cagily asked Ingrid, "Do we come back this same way?"

"Yes," she said. "Five miles up and five miles back down." That was all I needed to hear. I now saw my chance for a little rest and rehabilitation.

Sharon was walking along completely absorbed in her conversation with Eric, and everybody else was involved in struggling along, so nobody was watching me. Little by little I let myself fall back to the end of the line and then stood still until they were well out of sight.

The previous day I had seen some bushes with wild blueberries, and I was determined to pick and eat them and then meet the group again on its way down. I rushed to the first bush and began to pick and eat. Nothing before had ever tasted quite so wonderful to me, but I guess I'd never before been quite so hungry. I picked and ate and moved along, then picked and ate some more, neglecting to note my route. In half an hour I was totally lost.

Chapter Eleven

Suddenly I heard a low growl, looked up in disbelief, then froze in terror. A bear was standing about six feet in front of me, watching me eat his blueberries. And he obviously didn't like it.

Now bears were not something I ordinarily thought about back in Beverly Hills. However, I did know something about bears and what I knew I didn't like. The summer before I had gone to Yellowstone with Paula and her mother, and the ranger there had warned us to have nothing to do with the bears. Real ones were nothing at all like cuddly little brown teddy bears.

I'd had no idea there were bears at Sunnyasi, but right in front of me was this live one, and it looked at me as if fat girls were its favorite food. Trembling in fear, I slowly began to inch back, hoping he wouldn't notice that I was trying to escape. He did notice. He glared at me with those beady brown eyes and let out a low, cranky, rumbling growl. Instantly I froze again.

I stood there for a few minutes, covered with perspiration and dying for some water. I had to do something. Maybe if he wouldn't let me back up, he'd let me sit down. I started to inch slowly down toward the ground. Perhaps once I was in a sitting position I could back up and it wouldn't be so obvious that I didn't like being there. Or maybe if I sat still for a while he would think I was a rock and go away. I moved very, very slowly until I was finally seated. The bear watched and didn't move. I closed my eyes, hoping he'd disappear, then opened them again. He hadn't moved.

I had never been more uncomfortable. Despite the blazing heat, goose bumps had broken out on my arms. The sun was getting hotter and hotter as it rose, beating down like a hammer on my head. Gooseflesh in the sun! It sounded like the title of a romance novel. But I wasn't feeling romantic. I was feeling frantic. How far had I wandered from the main path? Would the group be able to find me? If and when they did, how could I escape from the bear? Perhaps when I heard their voices, I could let out a yell and make a run for it. I wasn't actually much of a runner, but maybe adrenaline would get me through when the moment came to sprint. Wanting to stay alive was a mighty powerful motivator.

No, it probably didn't make sense to run. He'd catch me in a second. I wouldn't run. Instead I'd just call out to tell them about my predicament and urge them to get a gun.

But would anyone at the fat farm have a gun? Was there anybody there who could shoot? After three days of starvation, did anyone even have the strength to hold a gun? Suppose they shot him and bits of him spattered all over me? Or suppose they shot him and he attacked me just before dying? Suppose they shot him and he fell on me? Oh, God, I thought, this is just ridiculous. I came here to lose weight, not my life.

I sat, and he watched. I could hear a brook flowing somewhere close, and yet I was dying of thirst. My lips were so parched that I could feel them beginning to crack. I kept licking them, but it didn't help much. I began to hallucinate the way people do in the desert, but what I imagined was not an oasis but our beautiful swimming pool back home in Beverly Hills. If I ever get out of this, I vowed, I'll never leave L.A. again. No bears in Beverly Hills.

I could feel my eyelids getting heavy, and I struggled not to fall asleep. My head kept jerking forward, and each time I would pull back in panic, thinking, if I fall asleep he'll eat me. But finally, I told myself, oh, the heck with it. It's better to be asleep when he's eating me than awake. And besides, sleep was the only remedy I could think of for my terrible thirst. The next time my head jerked forward, I sank gratefully into sleep.

When I opened my eyes, to my amazement it was dusk, and somewhere nearby I could hear voices calling my name. "Lois! Lois! Where are you?"

Nervously, I looked about me. No bear! I dragged myself up and simultaneously began to scream and hobble along. "Here! Here!" I screamed. "I'm here. I'm here."

I hurried in the direction of the voices and in a few minutes I saw the beams of flashlights and found a posse from Sunnyasi. "I'm here," I called in relief.

"Lois," my mom said, bursting into tears.

"Mom!" I also burst into tears. I threw my arms around her, and we couldn't stop hugging each other. Then we all started to hike back to Sunnyasi.

"Watch out for snakes," someone called out cheerily.

"Snakes!" Sharon yelped, grabbing at Eric.

"Don't worry," he said, putting his arm around her protectively. "I'm here! Usually they slither away when they see our lights. What happened to you, Lois? We've all been frantic with worry."

"*You've* been frantic!" While we walked I told them what had happened. In a short while we were back at the fat farm, and they gave me some soup in the dining room while I repeated my story for the group. To my surprise, nobody except Sharon and Eric seemed to believe me.

Chapter Twelve

Sonja, the owner, was absolutely furious with me. "I vill not haff you ruining our reputation," she growled. "There are no bears at Sunnyasi. There never haff been and there never vill be."

"Then what did I see?" I asked angrily.

"You saw nothing! You imagined! Perhaps you vandered avay and got lost and had to think up some kind of story. Perhaps you vent to search for fattening food. Perhaps you vent to meet somebody. I do not care vhere or vhy. Vat I do care about is that you haff vasted a day of everyone's time. And there are no bears!

"In fifteen years, we haff never had such a situation. You haff interfered with our routine. Instead of the serenity that our guests seek, you haff made everybody nervous and filled tension vith. Ve should haff known better than to take someone under eighteen, so spoiled and undisciplined, and so irresponsible. Ve only did it to oblige your mother. It vill not happen again.''

I was really angry at their disbelief and indifference to my fate. "What do I have to show you? Blood? I'm shocked that you don't believe my story. I am not a liar."

"Vat you are, my girl, is between you and your mother, but I vill haff to ask you to leave tomorrow."

"Leave tomorrow? But how can she leave?" Sharon asked. "I drove her here. There's no way for her to get home."

In the old days she could have phoned our chauffeur to come and get me.

"Ve vill drive her to the bus to Los Angeles first thing in the morning. You, of course, are velcome to stay."

"Now look," Sharon said, at her most charming, "I came primarily for her. I don't want to stay without her. Couldn't you please reconsider. I guarantee you that nothing more will happen."

"Absolutely no! Ve cannot lose another day of serenity. No discussion!"

Sharon was getting annoyed. "I've never heard anything so inflexible. If she goes, I'm afraid that I will have to go, too."

"As you vish! But ve vill not refund your money for this first week. You haff not yet paid for the second week, and ve vill easily fill your space. Ve always haff long vaiting lists. But ve cannot take guests in the middle of the veek, so you must be responsible in just the same vay as if you bought a subscription to the theater. This is vhy ve tell you that you are velcome to stay vithout her."

"I wouldn't dream of it! We're leaving immediately," Sharon said angrily. "I will not stay another night with such uncaring people. Look at her scratched legs. Look at her sunburned face. Look at her cracked lips. Listen to her voice. She's hoarse from lack of water today. We're lucky that she didn't get sunstroke. I haven't heard one word of sympathy for what she's gone through. What would she have to show you to elicit a little sympathy? Bear bites?''

"Ve haff no bears at Sunnyasi.''

"Very vell. I mean, very well. You will hear from my attorneys.''

Sonja was inflexible. A tough cookie! "As you vish. Ve might also consider suing you back for disrupting our schedule.''

"Well, we'll just see about that.'' In a fury, Sharon stormed out to pack. She was accustomed to getting her own way.

Eric hovered about, then carried our luggage out to our Mercedes. Sharon was in such a black mood that she hardly spoke to him.

"Hey, listen,'' he said, "I hope you're not angry because I'm staying. I'm not going to enjoy being here without you two, but I have to stay. I want to take off this potbelly in order to woo you.''

Sharon stopped stock-still, and the anger faded from her face. "Woo me?'' she echoed in a whisper.

He smiled at her. "Those are my intentions. What do you say?''

Her lovely eyes shone as he bent down and lightly brushed her lips with his. I sighed. It was so romantic.

"See you back in civilization,'' he said, closing her door behind her. Then he came around to my side and gave me a kiss. "You too, kid.'' He was really a nice guy.

She drove in a dream for a while, the smile still on her face. After a few minutes of savoring this wonderful turn of events, she said in a voice hushed with wonder, "Imagine that! How marvelously simple life is sometimes. What do you think of him, Lois?"

"I like him better than anybody you've met in a long time."

But gradually, as she drove, her mood shifted and she became more agitated with every mile. "It's a shame that I have to leave him there now," she worried. "Who knows who'll come up next week. Maybe someone young and gorgeous. Oh, Lois! I finally meet someone really eligible and I have to leave him to some other woman."

I was suddenly consumed with guilt. It was all my fault. "I'm really sorry, Mom. I never meant to interfere with your new romance. And I feel terrible about the wasted money."

Suddenly her lips turned up in an impish smile and her mood shifted again. "Don't worry about the money. I'd rather waste a month's fees than have to go through another week of that torture. To tell you the truth, the fun of roughing it ended very quickly for me, and I hate sixty-watt bulbs. I couldn't even see to tweeze my eyebrows."

"You big hypocrite! You kept acting as if you loved it and you didn't like it there any more than I did."

"I'm not a hypocrite. I'm an actress. And besides, I wanted to encourage you." Her face clouded up again.

"Don't worry about leaving Eric, Mom. You know he's not going to meet anybody more beautiful than you."

"You really think so?"

"I really know so."

I leaned my head lightly against her shoulder and slept until we were back at our wonderful, comfortable home. I hoped that maybe after this misadventure I would finally have a little peace about my weight.

"More wasted money," Missy commented the next day. "But I have another suggestion. I've just heard of a camp for fat teenagers where she should have gone without you. It's called Camp New Hope and it has several locations on each coast. It's coed and they guarantee to teach the right kinds of exercise and help kids develop self-confidence and learn to stay on a diet. It's especially designed for kids who feel left out at regular camp and feel unacceptable to peers. Of course, it is expensive—two to three thousand dollars for six weeks, but we had planned to spend that at Sunnyasi for the second week."

"Once and for all, Missy, will you butt out? I would have plenty of self-confidence if you and Sharon would just leave me alone. I am not unacceptable to all of my peers. In fact, a lot of them are more unacceptable to me than I am to them. And lastly, the whole idea of grouping fat people together gives me the creeps. Having nothing in common but your weight! Does anybody ever group thin people together? Do they assign you to bunks according to your weight? One bunk for a hundred and forty to fifty pounds, one bunk for a hundred and sixty to seventy pounds, and tents without running water to punish those who weigh over a hundred and seventy-five!"

"You always try to use your intelligence to get away with things," Missy said. "You might like that place."

"I'm not going to New Hope. Paula and I are going to lie next to the pool and search for the perfect diet.

And anyway, I'm going to Yosemite with her in August. I'll lose weight there.''

Missy shrugged in defeat, and Sharon drew her inside to tell her about Eric.

Chapter Thirteen

I phoned Paula first thing the next morning to tell her
I was home, then went down to breakfast. Sharon, sip-
ping black coffee and puffing away on a cigarette like a
steam engine, was having words with Marty, her agent.
"Everybody has ups and downs," he was telling her.
"Stop looking for the perfect part. It's always better to
work than not to. I'm warning you, stay away another
eight months and nobody will remember your name.
Take whatever I can get you and just bide your time
until the wheel turns round again for you."

"I don't have time to wait for wheels to turn. I might
be sixty by then. Joan Collins is still getting great roles,
and she's at least ten years older than I am. Maybe
twenty! I'm not much older than Sally Field or Meryl
Streep, and they're still getting great roles. And you
want me to take this nothing job in London."

"Comparisons won't get you anywhere. Take the London job. I guarantee something wonderful when you return. It's only a month. Maybe six weeks. Take the kid with you. Maybe she'll take off some weight with that rotten English food. What is it with you, kid? You have such a pretty face...."

"Why don't we talk about *your* personal appearance for a change, Marty?"

"You've got a funny kid there, Sharon. A real comedian."

He wouldn't let up. "Tell me the truth, kid. What is it? Some kind of oral fixation?" I looked at the gigantic cigar in his mouth and burst into laughter. He looked at me with hostility. He didn't like to be laughed at.

He turned back to Sharon. "Take the London job," he urged again, and finally Sharon grudgingly agreed. I was absolutely thrilled. It would be my very first trip to Europe. Paula had been in Europe many times. When her mother was in opera, she always took Paula along with her on tour. I quickly got dressed and drove to her house so she could tell me all about it.

She told me, "The best food in London is at Harrods. You can spend hours there cadging free samples. When we had a flat on Hill Street in Mayfair, we used to shop for groceries at Harrods, just as casually as we go to the Irvine Market."

Harrods is a famous department store, and on its first floor are great food halls with high, arched, tiled ceilings. You can find foods from even the most remote corners of the world in those halls.

"You have to try ox tongue," Paula continued. "It's much better than real beef tongue and it's not sold in the U.S. And fresh Stilton cheese! We don't get the same kind here. It's crumbly white with pale blue lines running through it. And the Godiva chocolate golf balls only cost about fifty cents over there.''

"What do you want me to bring you?''

"A big sack of different kinds of chocolates and Harrods' special name-brand cologne.''

Mrs. Lawrence came walking in, and I told her that Sharon wanted to go over on the Concorde.

"That's a wonderful idea,'' she warbled. "If the Concorde had been around a few years ago, I might not have retired. But I couldn't stand always being on planes and trains.''

I spent the entire day with them, learning about London. "The subway system is funny,'' Paula explained. "You buy a ticket when you get on and have to turn it in to get out. So don't lose it. I loved the subways. You can learn how to get around in one hour.''

I was almost crazy with anticipation, and finally, two weeks later we were off. "Are you worried about not seeing Eric again for such a long time?'' I asked Sharon.

"It's all right. I called him. He'll be waiting.''

"Oh, Mom. I'm really hoping!''

"I am, too.''

This was not only the first time I had gone to Europe. It was also the first time I had gone anywhere with Sharon. I'd spent more time with Mrs. Lawrence than with her.

Despite her continuing concern about the small role, she started to perk up when the stewardesses made a big fuss over her and asked for her autograph.

"Nobody's forgotten my name,'' she said, still bristling over Marty's words. "Maybe going to England will change my luck. Maybe I'll get some great offers and stay in Europe for a while. Europeans like older, more mature women like Catherine Deneuve. Or maybe I'll meet some marvelous, international tycoon and he'll insist that I leave the film business to help him entertain royalty. What do you think, Lois?''

"I kind of liked Eric, Mom. I'd rather have you settle down with someone like him.''

We reached Heathrow Airport in the late afternoon. The first thing I noticed was how many Indian workers there were sweeping all over the airport. It was kind of exotic. It really made me feel I was in a foreign country. "We have to try some Indian restaurants, Mom," I said.

"We're not eating any fattening food," she answered.

We stood in the passport line, which moved along quickly, and when we reached the passport official, he looked at Sharon's passport and squealed in an accent like the Beatles, "Sharon Long. I can't believe it. I've seen some of your old films on the telly. May I have your autograph?''

"Of course," she said graciously.

I've always thought it was a real pain to have to stop and give autographs, and I've never been able to figure out why people want them, but they do. And Sharon's always polite to fans.

"Here to make a movie?''

"Yes, I am!" She flashed her famous smile.

"Welcome to Merrie Olde England.''

We retrieved our luggage and moved out of customs into the airport lobby, and Sharon looked about for a limo driver. There were several in uniform, holding up signs with the names of passengers, but there wasn't one waiting for us. "In the past there was always a limo waiting for me," she said, close to tears.

"They probably sent one that just can't find us. Let's not waste time waiting here, Mom. There are a million things I'm dying to see. Anne Hathaway's cottage and Shakespeare's birthplace at Stratford-upon-Avon. And Piccadilly Circus and Portobello Road. Paula says I have to taste clotted cream and strawberries."

"We are not going to spend our time here eating," she answered automatically.

Just then, two women ran over to get her autograph, and instantly her expression of disappointment changed to the famous smile. They acted like she was their best friend.

"Wait till we tell people we saw you," they gushed. She stood there chatting with them for a minute, then, her spirits restored, she asked the porter to take us to a cab. People looked at her, noting how beautiful she was, even if they couldn't quite place her. The porter helped us into a cab, touched his hat and said, "Welcome to London, Miss Long."

His knowing also pleased her. That's one of the reasons I hate the movie business. Even though she was happy to be off to Europe with me, it wasn't enough for her. Being beautiful and thin, having a great house and having had a good career for a long time still weren't enough for her, either. She always had to be looking for approval and affirmation from total strangers, from people like passport officials and taxi drivers who meant nothing to her. It was possible that nothing would satisfy her. On the other hand, I had a feeling that if she could find love with someone like Eric, she wouldn't care so much about silly things.

Chapter Fourteen

All the way in from the airport Sharon carefully studied her face in a triple-strength magnifying mirror and skillfully reapplied her makeup. I settled back to watch the scenery, which was kind of drab and depressing. I began to worry that London might disappoint me, but when we reached the hotel, things got wonderful again.

Everyone made a big fuss over Sharon there. She didn't have to stand at a desk to register the way you do with most hotels. Instead, while a parade of robot bellhops carried our luggage up, a tall, severe, very formal man with a snooty British accent, who was dressed in a cutaway, seated us at a polished antique desk and presented the registration papers to her. The moment she had completed them, he asked us to follow him and personally escorted us to our room.

We took the elevator to the top floor, walked along a beautiful hallway with a curved ceiling painted in blue and white like Wedgwood china and entered a large, elegant corner room with a great view of Hyde Park. I whirled in delight. Thick carpets, thick enormous bath sheets and soft satin comforters. "I love it here, Mom."

"In the old days," she said, sighing, "they would have reserved a suite or half a floor for me."

In school we once read a Robert Frost poem called "Provide, Provide," which had lines that made me think of Sharon:

No memory of having starred
Atones for later disregard
Or keeps the end from being hard.

I tried to cheer her up. "We don't need all that space, Mom. I like the idea of sharing a room with you the way we did at the fat farm. This way we can talk late every night until we fall asleep."

She gave me a hug. "You're such a good kid, Lois. If only you weren't . . ."

"Please, Mom. Don't say it. Not now! I've had just about enough of that since the newspaper story came out. Let me enjoy London."

She sighed, then turned her attention to her set of matched Vuitton luggage. "In the past," she said, "a maid would have been waiting here to unpack for me."

"Oh, come on, Mom, we can unpack later. I have cabin fever from sitting on the plane all this time. I want to get out in the air. I want to ride on top of a double-decker bus."

She hugged me again. "All right! I'll send for a maid when we get back." And we set off to explore.

Sharon had a week off before shooting began, and we went all over London, even though she'd seen most of the tourist sights before. "It's fun seeing everything again through your eyes," she told me.

"We could do a lot more of this, Mom, if you retired. We've never really had enough time together. I've always wanted to go shopping with you instead of with Missy, or on vacations with you instead of Mrs. Lawrence, much as I love her. But you're my mother, and I like being with you."

"I like being with you, too," she said.

She wore low heels, sunglasses and a short wig during the days, and nobody recognized her. We went all over: to Westminster Abbey, St. Paul's Cathedral (which I recognized from *Mary Poppins*), Soho, on a boat up the River Thames to Windsor Castle, to see the changing of the guard at Buckingham Palace and to the Tower of London where the guide told us all about Anne Boleyn, one of the wives of Henry VIII. He cut her head off when he wanted to marry someone else. And as if that wasn't bad enough, *she* had to pay the executioner herself in order to make sure that he would do a nice clean job and not hurt her. What nerve! To have to pay your own executioner!

The Tower fascinated me, and so did the rest of London. Each day we had tea at a different place: our hotel, Fortnum and Mason, Brown's, Claridges, the Savoy, the Ritz. I had never really liked tea, but somehow in London, calmly sitting in a lovely setting and watching people walk by, tea tasted different from back home. And the scones with strawberries and clotted cream tasted just as good as Paula had said.

The following week Sharon began to work, and I was on my own, but I never felt lonely. London is an absolutely great city. You can walk all over. I never realized how much I missed walking and liked to do it until I was there. In Los Angeles we never walk. In Beverly Hills, if you're walking out at night, a cop pulls up and asks for identification, and even Rodeo Drive is only three blocks long. But in London you can walk for hours and there's always something exciting and new to see.

I followed Paula's instructions and spent a lot of time at Harrods Food Hall. Harrods confirmed my feelings about food as a fine art and showed me that there's nothing to be ashamed of if you're interested in food. When I walked through the halls, munching on Stilton cheese, ox tongue and the Godiva chocolate golf balls, I was totally happy. I felt proud of the human race because of how far we've come from cavemen in terms of the art of food. I stood gazing for ten minutes in awe at a perfectly symmetrical, perfectly balanced *croquembouche*, a topiary of caramelized cream puffs. It was a delicate, fragile work of art, and it interested me a lot more than stained glass.

Actually, I enjoyed the Food Hall more than Westminster Abbey or the National Gallery or the Tate Gallery. In fact, dumb as it may sound, I don't enjoy churches or museums all that much. I could do most churches in about five minutes, although it was interesting to see Canterbury Cathedral because I have a videotape of *Beckett*, with Peter O'Toole and Richard Burton.

I might have guessed that the peace was too good to last. One day I wandered down to the set where the paparazzi were taking pictures of Sharon, and they snapped one of me talking to her. It appeared in the paper the next day with the caption, "Sharon Long visits London with twin daughters."

Sharon is so thin and tiny that by comparison maybe it did look as if there were two of me. Or maybe they were just being funny. Sharon didn't find it amusing. That night she paced back and forth histrionically in our room shaking the paper at me. "How embarrassing! How humiliating! I'm a good mother and don't deserve this. Isn't that true?"

"You're a great mother! The best!"

"So why are you doing this to me? Why are you embarrassing me this way?"

"I'm not doing it to you, Mom. My body isn't your problem. It's mine!"

"Not true! All of my friends blame me. Missy blames me. They all say you're fat because you don't have a father."

"Oh, Mom. Why do you listen to them? Is every girl who does have a father thin? I can't bear amateur psychologists. They should worry about their own families."

"But the fact is, darling, that you are fat and I'd do anything to help you. I hadn't intended to get married again just yet, but I'll try to develop this relationship with Eric if that's your problem."

"That's *not* my problem. That's your problem. I don't have a problem and a father has nothing to do with it. I wouldn't have a problem if you would just let me alone. It's just what I am."

"But it's not what you have to be. If you make up your mind to it, you can get skinny. Look at all the celebrities who did. Just think of the joy of finally seeing bones. Well, we've tried the hypnotist and the analyst and Sunnyasi. We'll just have to think of something else when we get home again."

Sharon was really so humiliated that it cast a pall over the remaining time in London. I suppose I understood her point of view, but I also resented it. She's a celebrity, and I suppose she owes her public something. But I belong to myself. I don't think I owe being thin to strangers.

I kept a low profile for the rest of our time there, wandering around the city during the day and watching BBC, which I love, at night. One interesting thing that happened was that one day, in a secondhand bookstore in Tavistock Square near the University of London, I came across a book of stories about customs in various lands.

In one chapter, it said that in eastern Nigeria it is a sign of beauty and wealth to be sleek and fat. Part of a girl's initiation into womanhood is a custom called, "the fattening," in which the girl goes into seclusion to stuff on high-calorie foods.

What Sharon and her friends find so horrifying in L.A. is encouraged in Nigeria. Sometimes a girl is in the fattening room for two years, or as long as it takes to get adequately fat. When she finally emerges from seclusion, a public celebration is held in her honor and she's admired and treated as though she were a tribal chief. She's the source of a public celebration, not a public embarrassment!

I told Sharon all about this on our flight home.

"You see," I pointed out, "this emphasis on skinniness is not some kind of commandment handed down by God. It's just the custom of the country. And it wasn't even always the custom of the U.S. Have you ever seen pictures of Lillian Russell and Diamond Jim Brady? If I'd lived back then, I'd be on the cover of *Vogue*. I'd be the toast of the town. Or maybe the croissant of the town."

Sharon wasn't impressed. "I don't know where Nigeria is, and primitive tribal customs have absolutely nothing at all to do with living in Beverly Hills. No matter what that book says, I intend to take action. I owe it to you. Since you and Flash don't seem to hit it off with each other, the next step has to be joining a gym."

Chapter Fifteen

Paula and I spent the rest of the time before we went to Yosemite trying different diets. One, called the pasta diet, had us eating pasta three times a day. Of course we put on weight. Then we tried another diet, which is all fruit, and by day three we had diarrhea and were turning green. The next was a diet that promised that in seven days we'd lose up to twenty pounds. It told us what foods to eat, mostly baked potatoes and rice and bananas, and said we could eat until we were stuffed. Naturally, we didn't lose an ounce on that diet. We both put on weight.

Another diet instructed us to eat only when we were hungry.

"But I'm hungry all the time," we said in unison.

Thank goodness, we had a break from the food obsession when Paula, her mother and I went to the Ahwahnee Lodge at Yosemite.

To my delight, Sharon decided to go to France with Eric at the same time. "I'm taking three kinds of diet pills with me," she said, "so that I'm not tempted to eat at those marvelous restaurants." Can you imagine anything sicker than going to world-famous restaurants and not eating?

"What does this mean?" I asked. "Wedding bells?"

"We'll find out. I haven't spent a month continuously with anyone in years other than Missy and you. Either I'll come back engaged or not speaking to him. Now try not to give Missy a hard time when you get back from Yosemite."

"Do me a favor, Mom. Tell her the same thing."

Yosemite was paradise. I think it's my favorite place in the entire world. As soon as you enter the valley and see the meadows and high mountains and waterfalls, you start to feel good about life. Reverent! It's like a big outdoor cathedral in which people show their respect for nature. And the Ahwahnee Lodge was really beautiful. We had two adjoining rooms and a balcony that looked out over the marvelous mountains. We just stood there breathing the fresh pine air.

The first night we went to the Visitors' Center to see a one-man play about John Muir. He was a poor man who loved nature and fought to preserve Yosemite from greedy developers who wanted to flood the valley for electric power, and he founded the Sierra Club. It just made me shiver to think of something so magnificent and extraordinary as Yosemite almost being lost. And it was inspirational to see that one man could make a difference because he stood for something. He knew what he believed in and he fought for it. I thought that was the kind of person I'd like to be.

Mrs. Lawrence was as relaxed as usual. She let us do whatever we wished. If we didn't show up for meals, she ate alone or found someone to eat with, and she was perfectly cool about it.

Every day we hiked and rode bicycles all over the valley, gradually working ourselves up to the final eight-mile hike from Glacier Point.

We took a bus up there, stood gazing at the miles of beauty that lay beneath us and then hiked down. Even though most of it was downhill, it was the hardest hike I'd ever done. We carried knapsacks with trail mix, fruit and water, but we only stopped to drink. Somehow all of that heat and climbing left us without appetites. And hard as the hike was, it was different from hiking at Sunnyasi because we were cheerful, moving along at our own pace, resting when we felt like it.

It took us five hours, and we began to get worried toward the end because dusk was falling, but finally we emerged at Curry Village and took the free shuttle bus back to Ahwahnee. It was one of the best experiences of my life.

To my surprise, when we got back to L.A. Sharon was there, and she was in a foul mood, angry and depressed and looking for trouble.

"What happened?" I asked. "Where's Eric?"

Marty had phoned her about a part in a television movie and she had come right home.

"You mean you just left him in France?"

"Yes, and then when I got home, I found that the deal had fallen through."

"Oh, Mom. You shouldn't have done that. He was really special. I bet he wouldn't have done that to you."

At my words, she exploded. That's the way she always acts when she's feeling guilty. "I suggest you

worry about yourself, Lois, instead of criticizing me.
You've been away hiking for two weeks, and even so,
you still look awful. This cannot go on. You cannot
continue to look like this. Even behind the Iron Curtain women are beginning to look better. I told you in
London that the only thing that's going to work with
you is to go to a gym every day. That's what we're going
to do tomorrow."

"I hate exercise. I don't want to go. Everybody else
looks better than me in their leotards."

"You'll do exactly what I say, and I don't want any
further discussion. My problem is that I've never been
firm enough with you. You're joining a gym."

I marched to my room in indignation, and fifteen
minutes later, predictably, Sharon came up and apolo-
gized. "I'm feeling better. Marty just called. He has a
job coming up for me in New York. I shouldn't take my
disappointments out on you."

"That's right. You shouldn't. I'm getting sick and
tired of being your whipping girl every time your career takes a nosedive. Why don't you just retire and
marry Eric?"

"He hasn't asked, and he's probably angry at me for
leaving him. Besides, after a lifetime of working, I'm
afraid of the emptiness. I guess I could enjoy being a
full-time wife, but until I have that, I have to have a career." I didn't answer. "Still angry?" she asked.

"Oh, no," I said sarcastically. "I just love to be attacked for nothing. You think that the minute your
good mood is restored everything is peachy again. Other
people have feelings, too, in case you didn't know."

She put her arms around me. "I really am sorry. I
know I can be awful. Let's make a deal. I promise to
watch myself and never do that again and you promise

to go to the gym. So what do you say? Can we make a deal?''

It's hard to stay angry at Sharon when she's being charming. "All right," I said, sighing. "I'll go."

Chapter Sixteen

When I came down to breakfast the next morning, Sharon said, "I've made an appointment for you at the Beautiful People Gym. There was an article about it in *People* magazine. Everyone says it's the best."

"Oh, no," I protested. "I read that article. I don't want to go there. They won't even sign you up unless you're gorgeous, and all those beautiful girls only go there to meet guys. It's not really a gym. It's a singles' dating place."

"Don't be silly. Of course they'll sign you up. That's their business. And being surrounded by beautiful bodies will be an inspiration to you. Give it a chance. You'll see! You'll lose weight, look beautiful and get a boyfriend. By the time I was your age I'd been engaged three times."

There was no escape! After breakfast we drove to the gym and I found that my predictions had been correct.

Not only was everybody gorgeous, they all wore revealing leotards that were one inch away from nudity, and there I was schlumping around in my prison-gray warm-up suit. I wanted to hide.

A divinely beautiful hostess greeted us with, "Hi! I'm Cindy."

She showed us around and then sat us down with a contract. The initiation and registration costs for the first year were nine hundred dollars. "And she must have a private trainer," Cindy added. "That's another thirty-five dollars an hour."

My heart yearned for Yosemite, for exercise that meant something, for the beauty of nature that uplifted my spirits rather than this place, which was making me more depressed by the minute. I felt like Schwarzenegger in *Conan The Barbarian* when he was chained to the wheel.

"Mom, you've already spent too much on my body," I whispered. "Let's get out of here."

Ignoring me, Sharon said, "I'll pay anything necessary to get some results fast."

She left, and the receptionist buzzed for a trainer. A few minutes later a guy of about twenty came walking over to the desk, and Cindy said, "Jeff. This is Lois Long. Sharon Long's daughter."

"Oh, wow," he said. "Sharon Long!"

I looked at him, and my heart flip-flopped. Oh, wow, yourself! What a hunk! Blond, blue-eyed, perfectly built, friendly, with the kind of smile that made me feel like Christmas. A sun god! One of the handsomest men I'd ever met, and I've met plenty through Sharon. Love at first sight! Romeo and Juliet! Heloise and Abelard! Tristan and Isolde!

His clear blue eyes twinkled warmly into mine. "Follow me," he said.

I'll follow you anywhere, I thought. For the first time in my life I was in love. And if the one way I could see him would be to go and be trained every day, that was exactly what I'd do. Much as I hated exercise, I was going to make the sacrifice for him.

He pointed to the locker room. "I'll be waiting right outside for you," he said in one of the sexiest voices I'd ever heard. "Now don't keep me waiting."

In the locker room hordes of gorgeous naked girls were flitting about, blow-drying their hair and applying their makeup with wonderful unconcern. I looked at them with the same kind of wistfulness with which I'd watched the horseback riders at Will Rogers Park.

Sharon once said that inside every fat person is a thin person struggling to get out. Looking at all of those perfect bodies I saw no chance of the thin me ever emerging. It was just too far to go.

I was ashamed to change in front of all those stunning girls, so I just dumped my leotard in the locker and came back out in my warm-up suit, feeling inferior, inhibited and despondent.

Jeff was waiting right outside for me, dancing by himself to the loud background rock music and holding a clipboard.

"That was fast! This will be your chart. Ready? Let's go, babe. Today is the first day of the rest of your life."

He put his arm around my shoulders and led me to the scale. His touch made me tingle right down to my toes and gave me courage for the horrible ritual of the weigh-in.

"One seventy-five," he said. "That's not so bad."

"It's not?"

"Of course it's not. It's a challenge. We get loads of gals in here who weigh more than that."

"Really? Where are they?"

"All around you. They got thin. What you're looking at is not before, it's after."

"Are you conning me, Jeff?"

"Why would I do that? Don't be so suspicious. I can't con about weight. The scale is purely objective. It tells it how it sees it. So don't worry. We'll blast that weight off you. That's what we're here for."

Then he led me to the machines. "Very interesting," I quipped. "No iron maiden?"

"No! Only Nautilus. Lay down!"

I winced but said nothing, vowing that I would never under any circumstances criticize Jeff's grammar. The world said it was better to look like him and be ungrammatical than to be a blimp like me who knew the difference between a subject and an object. And besides, I wouldn't do anything to offend him.

The first series of machines was for the legs: body extension, leg extension, leg curl. First on my back, pulling the weight to my chest with my knees. Then on my stomach, pulling up my hamstrings. Then sitting and raising the weight and then sitting and pushing it back. Every time he touched my shoulder or showed me how to adjust a belt, I shivered. I couldn't wait to tell Paula about this surprising turn of events.

After the leg series came the arm series: pectorals, arm curl, arm extension, shoulder press, vertical chest and biceps curl, and then the abdomen series. After he'd shown me how to use each of them, noting the correct machine weight on my chart each time with the seriousness of a surgeon, he led me to the bicycles.

These bicycles were unusual because in the front, right beside the place where your speed, blood pressure, mileage and calories expended were listed, was a tiny TV.

Jeff explained what I should do, then said, "I'll be back for you in twenty minutes, kid. Go for it."

I started to pedal away furiously. The TV was a good distraction. Other bicyclists were wearing Sony Walkmans, grooving on rock, and lost in echo chambers of their own. I decided to bring one with French-langugage cassettes in it the next time I came, so I could improve my mind while pedaling away.

When he came back, he looked at the machine's computer to see how many calories I'd expended and where my blood pressure was.

"Not bad," he said. "Not bad at all. You'll be a jock yet, Lois baby. I promise you. I have to take off now. Do you feel up to joining the aerobics class?"

"I don't know. I've already done more exercise than in my entire life."

"Try it for me," he pleaded, as if this really meant something to him. "You can always leave if you find it too hard. Okay?"

"I guess."

Chapter Seventeen

Jeff led me into the aerobics class, which hadn't begun yet, and introduced me to the lean, gorgeous teacher.

"This is Lois, Pammy." He smiled, putting his arm across my shoulders again. "My main gal. Take good care of her."

"I sure will, Jeff." She beamed at him.

"Later," he said to me with a smile. Great dimples in his cheeks and a dimple in his perfect chin! My eyes followed him until he was out of sight, and then I turned to watch Pammy.

Just as we started to rotate our heads, I was startled by a rough push on my arm. "Move," a girl said to me. "You're in my space."

"What?"

"You heard me, fatso. That's my space."

I looked at the girl, who was pretty, thin, arrogant, and I got stubborn. "That's the most ridiculous thing I ever heard. Spaces don't belong to people."

Everybody else in the room was following the teacher's exercise gyrations, and I turned back to follow along. To my amazement, the girl pushed into my space and began to do the exercise, which involved bending the arms at the elbows and then flinging them back. And every time she flung hers back she managed to smack me.

I'm usually pretty slow to anger, but suddenly I felt more fury than I could remember welling up in me. How dare she come in late and expect to find a space waiting for her! How dare she call me fatso and try to push me around! We'd just see about that!

We were now making big circles with straight arms, and she kept hitting me. I felt like an angry machine as I rotated my arms around and around, and the next time she hit me, I swung back so hard that I knocked her to the floor. Bully for me! Take that, you nasty little twit. She sat there wailing.

The teacher turned off the cassette, and the entire class stopped and looked at us. "She took my space, Pammy," the girl wailed, "and knocked me down."

Everyone was looking at me angrily for having disrupted the class. "*Are* there reserved spaces?" I asked.

"Not exactly," Pammy said, "but some people like to stay in the same place each time they come."

"Suppose two people like the same space?"

"We're going to have to talk about that later. We're wasting time. Why don't you just move to the back of the room for now."

"Me? But I was here first. Why should I move? I'm paying just as much as anybody else here."

"I'm not used to this kind of thing," Pammy snapped, and she no longer looked so gorgeous to me. "Just move!"

The girl smirked and moved into my spot. Burning with a feeling of betrayal, I stalked out of the room in tears, resolving never to go back. I'd tell Sharon to stop the check immediately.

In my frantic flight, I bumped into someone and looked up to apologize. Oh, my God, it was Jeff. Just what I needed to complete another weight failure experience.

"Hold on there," he said, grabbing my arm. "Why are you crying? Did you get hurt?"

I shook off his hand, ran out of the building and stood in the street crying. "Tell me what happened," he said. "Who do you want me to kill?"

I clamped my lips tightly so I wouldn't say, "Whom." Suddenly I was laughing through my tears. "Some people are just so awful," I said, and I told him what had happened.

He laughed. "The territorial imperative! Just feel sorry for that little witch, Lois. There must be something wrong with someone who would make such a fuss about a spot on the floor. Maybe that's all she has. A spot. So don't take it personal. Like it's her problem."

I wiped my eyes. "I'm not coming back anymore."

He grabbed me by the shoulders and shook me gently. "You can't do that to me. I mean, like we're just beginning. I'll speak to Pammy, but you don't have to ever go back to that class anyway. There are lots of others for you."

When I didn't answer, because I was still so close to tears, he said, "Pleeese, Lois! I'm absolutely starving, but I won't go to lunch until you promise me you'll be here tomorrow. Pleeeese! For me! Promise!''

"All right." I finally capitulated. "I'll be here."

"And I'll be waiting."

For the rest of the day, whenever I wanted to reach for something to put in my mouth, I saw Jeff's luminous eyes before me, and I refrained. This was working in a way that hypnosis never had.

When I awakened the next morning, I lay in bed for a few minutes trying to remember why I was feeling so good. Then I thought of him, bounded out of bed, had fresh orange juice and a bran muffin and called Paula.

"Down, girl," she said. "All trainers are charming. That's their stock-in-trade."

"Don't be so cynical. He's not that way at all. Come with me today."

"Let me think about it. Pedaling around and around on a stationary bicycle for an hour to stay in the same place seems a little too boring and a little too symbolic for me this early in the morning."

I quickly drove to the gym for our appointment, and my heart began to pound like a bongo drum when I saw him at the desk, waiting for me. His smile bathed me in warmth. "There's my main gal," he sang out. "Let's go warm up."

"No scale?"

"Not today. There's too much daily fluctuation. It can be depressing. We'll weigh you again on Friday. And no machines today, either. The muscles need a day to rebound."

While Jeff began to teach me how to warm up each day, I noticed a man with a camera standing around snapping pictures of people. He hadn't been there the previous day.

"Who is that guy?" I asked.

Jeff shrugged. "I haven't the slightest! Probably someone doing PR for the gym."

"Well listen, could you like ask him to take pictures of someone else? I don't feel exactly gorgeous yet. Tell him to come back in a year or two."

"He's not taking pictures of you. He's just taking pictures of the club at random. Forget about him. Just concentrate on me."

Who could resist that kind of invitation? After we warmed up and stretched for ten minutes, he showed me how to use free weights. Every time he touched me to show me something I shivered as I had the previous day.

Then we did a number of exercises that I hated, such as the hydrant, the bicycle and push-ups. Whenever I wanted to give up, he pleaded with me, "Just do one more for me. That's right, Lois. Push! Now another." And miraculously he kept me going, even getting me to go up on my shoulders and put my legs over my head.

"And now," he said, "it's time for tag. Catch me, Lois." He tagged me, then ran out of the gym and around the block. I've always hated running, but I was determined to catch him. We went flying around and around the block. Finally he started to run backward, and with a final spurt of energy I caught and tagged him. It was the first time in my life I'd ever enjoyed exercise.

He looked at his watch. "Our hour is up. Now ride the bicycle for half an hour and I'll see you tomorrow."

Chapter Eighteen

On Friday Jeff led me to the scale as soon as I arrived.

"No, no, no," I said. "Use the water torture. Use cattle prods. Pull out my fingernails. Just don't make me weigh myself."

"Up," he said. "And stop talking. You weigh more with your mouth open."

"Is that true?"

"Of course not. Just get on the scale and keep quiet."

"Can I close my eyes?"

"Coward!"

I stepped on the scale with trepidation, closed my eyes and waited. Then he let out a low whistle. "Well, just look at that. One seventy. You're doing me proud. You've lost a pound a day, Lois. Now that wasn't hard, was it?"

I felt as if I'd received an Academy Award. "I owe it all to you."

"Damned straight you do. And don't you forget it. Come on, kid, let's go celebrate. I'll take you to Duke's for lunch. My treat."

Duke's is this real funky little place on Santa Monica, where everybody hangs out. The food sucks, but it has great vibes. It's like a little club for people moving up in the industry, kind of the way I imagine Schwab's Drugstore was when Lana Turner was discovered there. Maybe Duke's replaced it as an inexpensive hangout. Jeff ordered an avocado and sprouts salad on whole wheat pita and iced tea, and I ordered the same.

It was the first opportunity we'd really had to talk and learn something about each other. He'd come to L.A. to look for work as an actor and was working at the gym while he looked. His father owned a drugstore in Ohio, his mother taught elementary school, his older sister worked with his father as a pharmacist and his younger brother was in high school. "*Bor*ing!" he said, dismissing his family with a wave of his hand.

"Do you like living in L.A.?" I asked.

"Sure I do. Anyone who doesn't like Hollywood is either crazy or sober."

We laughed together at that, and then he asked about *my* family. He wanted to know everything there was to know about me and about Sharon, but I never felt as if he were prying. Just interested! A lot of people think that actors lead exciting, glamorous lives, and I guess he did too at first.

"She's never had much fun," I told him, "because she's been working since she was fifteen and she's always had to take such good care of her face and figure. We met this man, Eric, at the fat farm, and I really liked him. I thought they had something big going, but she left him in France for some dinky little role that fell through. I hope he forgives her. I wish she would marry, retire and live happily ever after."

He thought about what I was saying, then said, "I understand where she's coming from. The only way to get ahead in this town is to give it your all. When I get through at the gym, I take voice, dance and acting lessons. And three times a week I go for the Alexander Technique."

"What's that?"

"It teaches you how to move, how to carry your body. It would be good for you, too. Teach you to carry yourself like a queen. It's a way of eliminating unnecessary tension while learning to move in an easier and more effective way. My teacher works with the members of the L.A. Philharmonic."

"That's really interesting, Jeff. I never realized that musicians have to be concerned about movement and posture. Now that you mentioned it, I see how logical it is."

Then I explained my school situation to him. "If I continue to lose weight, my mom will let me stay in my school and then I can still come to the gym after school. But if I don't lose weight, it's off to private school with me so I won't embarrass her, and you and I couldn't continue to work together."

He looked deep into my eyes. "I wouldn't like that."

"Neither would I."

He kept bringing the conversation back to Sharon. He wanted to know how she got her start, who her agents were, where she'd studied, what her favorite films were. Nothing connected to Sharon or "the industry" seemed trivial to him.

"Do you think I could meet her sometime?" he asked.

"Sure. It's no big deal. Come over to swim with us on Sunday. You have to meet her this month because next month she'll be in New York."

"How's Sunday afternoon?"

"Great! I'll tell Sharon and invite my friend Paula and we'll have a barbecue next to the pool."

"Sounds great to me, too."

But Sharon had other plans. "I'll meet Jeff some other time. Please tell him for me that I think he's doing a great job with you and I'm very pleased about that. Eric's back from France, and we're spending the weekend at the San Ysidro Ranch. You kids have a good time together, and please include Missy."

"I promise. You tell her to be pleasant to Jeff, please. This is important to me."

The San Ysidro Ranch is a famous romantic place in Santa Barbara.

"If he pops the question, Mom, say yes."

"I'm thinking about it."

We were both happier that day than in a long time. Both of us were feeling full of hope.

Our cook is off on Sundays, but Paula and I wanted to cook anyway. We worked all morning preparing coleslaw, jicama salad and cucumber salad in the Cuisinart. We put chickens and steak in to marinate and bought jumbo shrimps and eggplant in garlic at the Irvine Market. For dessert we hollowed out half a watermelon and filled it with fresh strawberries, fresh pineapple chunks, kiwi and melon balls.

Missy walked by clucking her tongue. "I can't believe you're preparing this much food for one guest."

"It's for all of us. You too, Missy. We're going to have a great party."

When I heard his motorcycle in the driveway, my heart began to pound wildly, and I ran out to meet him. He got off his bike, looked at the house and let out a low whistle of approval. That always embarrasses me. I hate to have people get all impressed by the house. It's judging again by externals, the same way that people look at fat people.

"Nice house," he said weakly.

"Now all we have to do is pay for it," I joked, because I thought that would make him feel better. "Come on out to the pool. Paula and I are starving."

He followed me through the house, examining each room with admiration. "What a pad! Is your mother out at the pool?"

"No, and I'm really sorry. I wanted her to meet you. But she had to go away this weekend."

For a moment he looked terribly disappointed, then he flashed me his wonderful smile, put his arm around my shoulders and said, "Oh, well. At least you're here."

I could have died of happiness!

Chapter Nineteen

It was a great day. It wasn't that we did anything so special. We swam, laughed, talked, barbecued, ate. But I felt so normal, so happy, so hopeful. Everything flowed. Jeff charmed Paula and Missy just as much as he'd charmed me. He had one of those great, easy personalities that brought out the best in everyone.

"You're right," Paula whispered to me. "He is a fox."

Even Missy liked him. He convinced her to come into the pool, the first time I'd seen her do that in five years, and to join us in a game of water polo. She looked younger, flushed, cheerful.

"Don't think," he said, "that just because you're thin, Missy, you don't have to do some exercise. You have to tone your muscles to keep that body beautiful even though you're past thirty."

Paula and I looked at each other. Missy would never again see thirty unless she was reincarnated. Was he conning her or just being nice? I thought he was being nice, and it made me like him even more.

He even got her to promise to join the gym. "Trust me," he said, smiling into her eyes. "Look how well Lois has been doing."

"You're right," she said. "I thought she was a hopeless case. You're the first person who's ever gotten through to her."

I threw her an indignant glance, but Paula grabbed my wrist. "Ignore her," she whispered. "He's just shining her on. It's his business."

But Paula, too, was not immune to his charm. He listened intently while she told him about her mother's attitude toward weight and then he said, firmly but nicely, "That's changing, too. We have a lot of singers who come to the gym, and they're not fat. Fat is old-fashioned. Strength is what you need to sing, not bulk. Can I be frank with you, Paula?"

"Sure! I guess so! Why not?"

"When I look at you, I don't see the present you. I see you ten pounds thinner, with a few muscles, and you're an absolute knockout. I'd like to get you there. Please don't think it's just business. I care about people! I really do! I like to spread happiness, and attractive people are happy people. When you look good, you feel good. It's as simple as that."

All three of us beamed at him. He certainly was making us happy. Especially me! The weather matched our mood. No smog, balmy breezes and friendly, caressing sun.

We fluttered about him like moths around a light bulb. After we got out of the pool, we sat and watched him execute perfect dives until Paula and I began the barbecue.

When the food was ready, Jeff gave me a little glance to remind me. I took very small portions and chewed slowly, forcing myself not to notice how heartily they were all eating. He smiled his approval at me. "That's my main gal." I didn't care if I ever ate again.

We spent the rest of the day running old films of Sharon's on the VCR and it was fun to see them again through his eyes. "They just don't make musical comedy stars like that anymore."

"They don't make musical comedies like that, either." Missy sighed. "That's one of Sharon's problems. They film a punk rock concert instead and call that a musical. When they make a musical, it's peculiar. And Sharon doesn't want to tour in a stage revival."

"But she really was great," he said admiringly. "She had her time in the sun. No one can take that away from her. Most people aren't that lucky."

The moon was up when he left. We walked him out to his motorcycle, he kissed us each on the cheek, and we watched him roar away. "So what do you think?" I asked them.

"A nice young man," Missy said wistfully, and suddenly I felt compassion for her. I saw that all of the girlish joy she'd shown during water polo had left her eyes.

"Missy," I asked impulsively, "why haven't you ever married?"

"Never found anyone I liked enough."

"But didn't you want a family?"

"I have a family. You and Sharon are my family. And I suppose you might say I'm married to my work."

Bigger is Better 107

How very sad, I thought. I put my arms around her and gave her a quick kiss on her dry cheek. "Thanks for being so nice to Jeff," I said. "Good night, Missy."

She looked at me in amazement. "It seems to me that he's affecting more than your weight." She gave me a little smile and waved good-night to us.

Paula and I lay awake for a long time that night talking about him. "You think he's wonderful, too, don't you?" I asked.

"Yes, but..."

"But? But what? What are you trying to say?"

"He's too nice. Too accommodating. Too good to be true!"

"Oh, come on, Paula. That's just plain ridiculous. Why are you so suspicious?"

"I don't know exactly. He's kind of like a pitchman on late-night TV selling a set of knives or some other product. There's something kind of fake about him sometimes. He smiles too much. I just felt he was playing a role all day."

"But why would he do that? He doesn't have to bring in business to the gym. It's probably full-up right now."

"I don't know. Maybe I'm wrong. I hope I'm wrong. It's just a kind of gut reaction. Don't pay any attention to me. It's just that my father left me suspicious about men's motivations."

Why do people always think gut reactions are correct? I'd rather go with an intellectual reaction than a gut reaction. I put my pillow over my head and went to sleep. Much as I adored Paula, I didn't want to listen to her saying anything bad about Jeff. It seemed disloyal somehow.

And when I saw Jeff at the gym the next day, I was glad I hadn't shared her opinions. Everything was just the way it had been the previous week. He thanked me for a great day and continued to work with me as he had before.

That man was still hanging around taking pictures but by now I hardly noticed him.

Chapter Twenty

Eric and Sharon came home Monday night, and what I had hoped for had come true. They were engaged. "Oh, Eric," I said, throwing my arms around him. "If I could have picked a father, it would have been you. When are you getting married?"

"At Christmastime," Sharon said. "When I finish that job in New York. After that, Eric wants me to take it easy for a while."

"So you'll move in here with us?" I asked him.

"No," Sharon said. "We have to buy a new house. Eric doesn't want to stay in *his* house. It has sad memories for him of his wife. And he doesn't want to move into our house."

"Why not?" I protested. "I love this house."

"Because it's your house," he said gently but firmly, "not our house. I want us all to start out together. New family! New home! But don't worry, Lois. We won't buy any house that you don't like.''

"I wish we didn't have to change."

He ruffled my hair affectionately. "People who don't change and move forward move backward. It's not possible to just stand still."

"Be happy, darling," Sharon said. "I am."

I hugged her. "You know I am, Mom."

But I lay in bed that night unable to sleep. Half of me agreed with Eric. You had to keep moving and changing. Wasn't that exactly what I was trying to do with Jeff? But the other half of me didn't want to. It had never occurred to me that we'd have to leave our house. Still, overall, I really was happy. We'd be a real family again, and I was willing to trust them.

Everything seemed perfect. Sharon had found a wonderful, rich new husband. I was getting thin, and I was certain I'd be able to return to Beverly Hills High in September. And maybe I had also found a boyfriend.

My thoughts were interrupted by a little knock on the door. "It's me, Missy. Can I come in and talk to you for a minute, Lois?"

"Sure!" What on earth did we have to talk about? I wondered. I looked at her face and saw that she had been crying.

"What's the matter?" I asked.

"I won't be living with you any longer after the marriage."

"Why not?"

"Sharon and Eric say that she'll no longer need a live-in secretary. I'll still work for her, but they think I should get a place of my own."

I thought of all the times I'd wished she would disappear, and I felt a little guilty. "Can you afford it?"

"Oh, yes. It's not financial. I haven't paid rent all these years and I've been putting my money away."

"Then what is it?"

"I thought you and Sharon were my family." She covered her face with her hands and began to weep silently.

"We are," I said. "We always will be. You know that. But I bet you'll love living away from us." And I told her what Eric had said about moving forward.

"You've worked hard for Sharon all your life. Now you should start thinking about yourself. When you were in the pool with Jeff, you seemed so happy and girlish and free. All these years, you've shouldered Sharon's burdens. I think you should be ecstatic about having time now to live for yourself."

She stopped crying and looked at me. "Do you really feel that way, Lois? You're not just trying to make me feel better?"

"One thing you know about me, Missy, is that I never lie. I'll tell you what Jeff told me the first day at the gym. He said it was the first day of the rest of my life. That's how you should feel about this change."

"Maybe it will work out all right." She sighed. "And I am happy for Sharon. She said you'll be her maid of honor and I can give her away."

I looked at her plain, worn face and suddenly felt as if she were a noble soul. Sharon was rich and beautiful and loved, but Missy didn't seem to feel an ounce of jealousy. And I felt guilty about how Paula and I always made fun of her name, Missy Booher. It occurred to me that most of my sensitivity had always been re-

served for me. Repentant, I gave her another hug. "I'm
sure it will work out fine," I assured her again.

Everything continued to go along well, and by the end
of the second week I was down to one hundred and
sixty. But I should have known there was a worm in the
apple. Paula and I were lying beside the pool one day
when Sharon came in shrieking in rage with a copy of
the *National Enquirer* crackling in her hands. "How
could you do this to me?" she screamed. Missy came
running out to see what she was upset about.

There, on the front page, was a big, glamorous picture of Sharon, and right below it was a picture of Jeff
and me at the gym. Jeff looked handsome and charming, of course, but I looked like a sweating elephant in
my gray warm-up suit. The headline said, "Star's
Daughter Sheds Fat."

"Did you know about this?" Sharon asked me.

"Of course I didn't," I said indignantly. "Do you
think you're the only one who doesn't like to be publicly embarrassed? I didn't know about it, and Jeff
didn't, either. A photographer's been hanging around
the club taking pictures. We thought he was doing PR
for the club. We didn't know he was looking for a story.
I'm sure Jeff will be furious."

"I'll sue that club," Sharon stormed.

Missy took the newspaper and started to read the article. Then she looked at me sadly and said, "Jeff did
know about this. In fact, I think he set it up."

"That's impossible. I don't believe you. How can you
say such an awful thing?"

"Because he quoted me." She read aloud. "'Sharon
Long's secretary claims Jeff Fields is the only person
who's ever been able to help Lois Long's weight problem. Formerly with the Beautiful People Gym, he has

now set up his own consulting service to work with similar hard-core cases."

I burst into tears. "That Judas. That snake in the grass. We should take out a contract on him."

"Don't feel bad," Missy said. "We were all taken in."

"What on earth is going on here?" I heard Eric ask, and Sharon held up the newspaper to him. He read the article, then said, "An opportunistic young man, it appears."

He put his arms around me while I sobbed, "I'm so ashamed. My heart is broken."

"There, there," he tried to comfort me. "Nobody gets through life without a broken heart. But it mends again, I promise you that."

I continued to sob. His words were kind, but they didn't make me feel better. "Being a straight-A student certainly hasn't made me smart about people."

"Nobody else would have been smarter in this situation," he said gently. "Con men count on the innocent to help them. So don't be so hard on yourself. In a week this will be old news."

"That won't take care of the situation," Sharon snapped. "Her heart is broken, and mine doesn't feel too good, either. The only solution is to send her to a good private school where they have barbed wire and machine guns to keep out photographers. I can't keep up with her weight any longer. I've been spending a fortune for absolutely no results. The more I spend, the worse it gets. I'm sick of worrying about it."

"Not any sicker than I am," I said angrily. "How do you think I feel about that awful story?"

Paula was as upset as I. "Please don't separate us, Sharon," she begged. "Say something, Lois. Tell her not to separate us."

"I don't care about that or anything," I mumbled, too humiliated to fight for anything. My face was flushed with shame. I'd been so happy, and it was all based on lies. How could I have been so gullible? Jeff hadn't cared about me. All he'd wanted to do was use me for publicity purposes because I was Sharon's daughter. And what made me feel the absolute worst was the fact that, for a little while, he'd made me hope.

"I don't want to talk," I said. "I'm too tired and upset. So just leave me alone. I don't care where I go to school. I don't care about anything anymore. You'll find another friend, Paula, who isn't such a gullible fool."

I ran up to my room, locked the door and looked in the mirror with disgust. How could I ever have thought Jeff liked me? No other boy ever had. I knew the way they talked about fat girls—pigs, cows, slobs, elephants. The boys at my school only wanted to be seen with thin, attractive girls. But I had thought Jeff was different.

He wasn't different. He was worse! I really hadn't expected him to care as much for me as I did for him. I could have accepted that. But he didn't have to use me, to betray me. He didn't have to humiliate me. What he had done indicated total and utter contempt for my feelings, for my personhood. It made me cringe.

Paula knocked on my door. "Please let me in, Lois," she called. "If you don't I'll go outside and climb in through the window. If I get killed it will be your fault."

"All right," I grumbled, unlocking the door.

She sat down on the bed and looked at me with concern. "You're not going to do anything stupid, are you?"

"Like what?"

"Like kill yourself over that male slut."

"Of course not! He's not worth it, and besides, suicide hurts. But I feel awful about it. You were right and I was dumb. I really thought he liked me, that we were friends. But it was all business! All an act! He used me to get ahead. That's the part that hurts."

"I think he really did like you as much as he was able. And I'm sure he didn't really want to hurt you. But you know this town. People do lots of things they don't want to in order to survive. My mom told me it used to be like that, too, in the opera world. Anything for the career!"

"I'll never accept that kind of behavior. It's wrong! I feel betrayed!"

"I'll never betray you, Lois." She put her arms around me, and I cried again.

"Hey, here's a joke to cheer you up," she said. "The optimist says that this is the best of all possible worlds and the pessimist answers, I'm afraid you're right."

"That really is a good one," I said, but even the joke couldn't console me that day.

Suddenly I was ravenous. "I'm hungry," I said. "Let's go eat."

By the time I went away to school in September, I'd put back all of the weight I'd lost with Jeff. Back to square one!

Chapter Twenty-One

The Radclyffe School, about four hours north of L.A., is one of the most exclusive boarding schools in the state. You can't even get an interview unless your family is prominent, and even then, there's no certainty of admission. It admits only two hundred girls and the cost is fifteen thousand dollars a year.

Of course, once they heard Sharon's name over the phone, we had no problem getting an appointment for an interview, but I knew they might change their minds when they saw me. Since Jeff's betrayal, I was not only fatter than before, I was now a lot less cheerful, a lot less trusting. My expression was certainly not optimistic.

Sharon and I drove there for the interview. A guard at the gatehouse checked off our name and then waved us forward onto a beautiful green campus. It was awesome! I loved it the moment I saw it. Hills, flower beds,

old trees, rolling lawns, a scene out of a romantic
dream, a garden paradise! Ivy-covered stone buildings
in a quadrangle around a flower-lined courtyard. Rus-
tic benches scattered about on perfectly manicured
grounds.

A small, discreet sign pointed the way to the admin-
istration building, a white, shingled structure with black
shutters where a thin, pretty, smiling girl was waiting for
us at the door. "Hi," she said. "I'm Julie Lowell, and
I've been assigned to you for today. Go right on inside.
Mrs. Vance is waiting for you. First door on your left.
I'll be out here to show you around when you get
through."

Following her directions, we entered an elegant wood-
paneled library where a white-haired woman with china-
blue eyes, a pink-and-white complexion and a serene
face was seated on a couch covered in floral chintz.

"Welcome," she said with a warm smile. She mo-
tioned to us to sit down as a uniformed maid wheeled in
a tea cart and then closed the door behind her. "Milk
or lemon?" Mrs. Vance asked in a low, well-modulated,
cultured voice. Sharon took lemon, although I think she
would have preferred a vodka and tonic, and I took
milk.

"Please help yourselves," Mrs. Vance said, motioning toward the tea table, which had wonderful foods on
it. There were little finger sandwiches of cucumber,
smoked salmon, tongue and turkey, and tiny miniature
strawberry and blueberry tarts with just a drop of cus-
tard inside them. Sharon threw me a warning glance not
to act like a pig, so I forced myself to eat slowly, the way
Jeff had taught me. Oh, Jeff! I forced back my tears.

After we'd been served, Mrs. Vance started to tell us
about the school program, and it sounded excellent. All

of their graduates went on to good colleges for which they were very well prepared academically. Classes were seminar-style with no more than ten students at a time, and they were academically rigorous.

Everything was individualized at the school for maximum learning: individual tennis lessons, riding lessons, golf lessons, language tutoring, music lessons, etc. Each student had her own room, and there was a bath between every two rooms. There was also maid service to make the beds and clean the rooms twice a week.

School trips were made at every vacation break: to Cuernavaca to study Spanish, to Aix-en-Provence to study French, to Italy to study art, to London for a week of theater-going, to Greece and Egypt to study ancient civilizations.

"It is our hope," Mrs. Vance said in her impressive, well-modulated voice, "that every girl graduating from here will have the manners, deportment, intellect and social skills needed both by successful career women and the wives of successful men. Two of our girls are married to ambassadors and one is vice president of a bank in New York."

We spoke about general things for a while and then she zeroed in on me. "Your grades for the first two years of high school are excellent and the recommendations from your teachers are also outstanding, other than in physical education."

"I never liked exercise," I mumbled.

"Here," she said, "you would be expected to participate in all aspects of school life. Is there any sport you like?"

"Swimming, I guess."

"Fine. Our indoor pool is modeled on the one at Hearst's San Simeon." We talked casually for a while and then she asked, "Do you think you would like to come here?"

"Yes. I think I would."

"Very well. But I must make certain facts clear to you. We are dedicated to the idea of a sound mind in a sound body. Both the inner and outer aspects of a person are of importance. You evidently have the intellect and character we look for, but your appearance is not the Radclyffe image. I wonder, Mrs. Long, if you have any thoughts about how we might go about improving Lois's appearance."

Sharon hesitated, concerned about saying the wrong thing. In her face I could see a combination of awe and wistfulness. She hadn't even finished high school, and I knew that this kind of old-money, finishing-school environment made her a little uneasy. I reached out and took her hand. I didn't want her to be intimidated by Mrs. Vance or anyone else.

"Perhaps you could put her on a diet," Sharon said, "or maybe there's a local chapter of Weight Watchers. Maybe someone on campus could watch what she eats. I know she'd like to be thin."

I sat there wincing at the way they were talking to each other about me as if I were in another room.

"If she just exerts a little discipline, the weight should come off easily. Our chef is quite conscious of health. We grow our own fruits and vegetables and our kitchen serves excellent low-calorie foods like whole-grain cereals, yogurt and skimmed milk. But she would have to discipline herself! We operate on the honor system here. We don't check books out of the library because everyone is honor-bound to replace them, and we don't lock our doors. We have never had a case of theft or cheating, although all examinations are unsupervised. It would be the same with dieting. She would have to be on her honor."

She turned to me with a warm smile. "Do you think you could do that? Discipline your appetite?"

She was the kind of person you wanted to please. Her sweetness and graciousness brought that out in me. I also wanted to be completely honest. "I would try. I really would. I developed some willpower this summer, but then I slipped back. Maybe I could do it again. I would certainly try."

She smiled at me approvingly. "Very well, my dear. Nobody can say more than that."

She stood up. The interview was at an end. "Julie will show you both around," she said, "and I will be in touch with you once I've discussed your case with the Admissions Board. I'd like to have you here, Lois. I'll present a very good case for you."

"Oh, God," Sharon muttered, dragging me into the ladies' room outside. "You'd think they were paying us, not the reverse. So what do you think?"

"I love it here. It's not hectic and jazzy like L.A. They have gardens instead of malls."

"You do? I've never felt more uncomfortable in my life. That woman made me feel overdressed, over-made-up and undereducated. I can't wait to get back to L.A."

I looked at her and grinned. She was wearing stiletto-heeled short boots, a beige suede miniskirt suit, her gold Rolex, large gold earrings, half a dozen gold chains and two rings, including the enormous sapphire and diamond one Eric had just given her. Her streaked brown hair had been crimped and stood out from her head like a tawny lion's mane.

"You look great, Mom. You always do. It's just a different style here."

"You can say that again. Squaresville! I haven't seen anybody dress that dowdy since that old Bette Davis movie, *Now, Voyager*. It would be too dull and quiet here for *me*."

"But I like it here. So much green. And those old trees. And I thought Mrs. Vance was wonderful. Kind of timeless, in a way. So quiet and serene. If they accept me, I'd like to come."

"It's a big investment if you change your mind in the middle of the year. Perhaps we should look at some other schools."

"No! This one's fine. You and Eric will just have to find a house without me."

"We'll look, but I promise you we won't settle on one until you've seen it."

When we came out of the ladies' room, Julie was waiting for us, and she showed us everything: the immaculate dorms and dining room, the marvelous library and the athletic facilities. "I've been here for a year now," she said when she escorted us to our car, "and I love it. I hope you decide to come, Lois. Maybe we could share a suite."

"Lovely manners," Sharon said. "When I see these kids, I wish I could live my life over again and go to good schools. Well, I can't go back in time, but I can see that you have the things I didn't have. That's why I never pushed you to get a little job when Missy advised it. I've worked too long. Enough for both of us. It makes you grow up too fast."

"You have given me the best, Mom. I feel bad that you've wasted so much money on me. The analyst and the hypnotist and the gym. I promise that if I get in here, I'll do everything right, including losing some weight.''

We drove back to L.A. singing happily along with the radio. Sharon was softer than I had ever known her to be. Eric was having a wonderful effect on her. For the first time since Jeff's betrayal I was feeling all right again.

Chapter Twenty-Two

Paula and I spent every afternoon together before I left for school, visiting all of our old haunts: the antiques shops along Melrose, Fred Segal where we liked to buy clothes and have lunch, and the Max Factor museum and makeup outlet on Highland Avenue.

We wandered through the museum looking at cosmetics and photographs of beautiful actresses from 1904 to today, then stocked up on discounted perfume and cosmetics. While we were there, two busloads of sight-seeing senior citizens pulled up, and they started to go crazy buying little thirty-nine-cent samples of mascara, blush-on, foundation and rouge for next Christmas's stocking stuffers. If they could bop around being so cheerful and chipper, there had to be hope for everyone.

But my mood changed as we walked along Hollywood Boulevard, which is a lot different from Rodeo

Drive. Like another world, really. "People sure look like freaks here," Paula said.

She was right. Hollywood Boulevard is filled with disturbed people talking to themselves, old people tottering along with groceries, transvestites, prostitutes, disabled people in wheelchairs or limping along on crutches, and fat people. I watched some of the other fat people walking along the Boulevard, looking down at the stars embedded in the ground, and it hurt me that they all seemed so unhappy. When you're fat and want to be invisible, you adopt a strange kind of I'm-not-here walk, with your eyes focused far off into the distance as if avoiding direct eye contact means that people can't see you. Kind of an ostrich approach to life.

"Why so suddenly quiet?" Paula asked. "Are you nervous about going?"

"Yes. Nervous and depressed. I don't want to be a freak at the school. And I hate leaving you. We're not going to grow apart, Paula, are we?"

"Of course not. I'll call you as much as possible. My mom doesn't care if I run up phone bills. And maybe I'll write, too."

"And I'll be home for Thanksgiving and, of course, for the big event at Christmas." Paula and Mrs. Lawrence were invited to the wedding.

"No one will ever take your place," we promised. But the truth of the matter was that we were both a little worried. "Remains to be seen." We grinned at each other as we said goodbye.

The next morning Sharon and Eric drove me to school where we found something terribly disappointing. That charming Mrs. Vance had unexpectedly retired at the end of August and been replaced by Patricia

Trainor, a graduate of West Point, who believed that discipline was the meaning of life.

When we appeared in her office, she looked at me with undisguised dismay. Apparently nobody had bothered to inform her that one of her new charges represented everything she associated with the decline of civilization. If we had not already paid, I would have turned around and gone right home.

From her expression, it seemed to me that she was equally dismayed by Sharon who was wearing beige silk pants, the usual high heels and a matching beige silk blouse opened all the way to her waist so that you could see lots of cleavage covered by gold chains. Her Joy perfume filled the room.

"Well, goodbye, darling," Sharon said, hugging me. Her eyes were moist. The first time I had ever been away from home!

Eric also gave me a big hug and told me, "We promise not to buy a house until you see it. If we find something we really like, we'll call you to come home."

After they'd gone, I flopped down on the couch, and Ms. Trainor looked at me with ice-gray eyes. "I have been reading Mrs. Vance's notes on you," she said coldly, "and I have put you into a connecting room with Julie Lowell. She's disciplined and slim. We feel she will be a good influence on you. I expect you to take off twenty pounds by Thanksgiving."

"I'll do my best," I mumbled.

"That's not good enough. No equivocation. Don't say, 'I'll do my best.' Say, 'I'll do it.'"

I hesitated. "Say it," she repeated.

I shrugged. Might as well give this nut what she wanted. "Okay, I'll *do* it."

"That's the spirit! Very well! Dismissed!"

Despondent, I went to find my dorm room. The doors to the bathroom and the connecting room were open, and Julie came running through them as soon as I got in. "I'm so glad you're my roomie," she said with a glow. Her enthusiasm immediately made me feel better.

Julie came from a really classy family. Her father used to be ambassador to Yemen, and since his return he had been angling for a Supreme Court appointment. "You think *you* have to be careful about publicity," she said after we got to know each other. "It's far worse with us. We can't ever do anything. We can't even breathe in public."

In Yemen she and her sister had never gone out of the embassy compound, had private tutors and never mingled with the people. They had never made a step without bodyguards, and their car was as strong as a tank for protection against bombs and bullets.

"Can you imagine what it's like to always be surrounded by men with machine guns? The child of a friend of ours was kidnapped for ransom, and they sent back his ear first as an inducement to move fast. My mother's so nervous about something like that happening to us that she drinks too much."

"Well, it must be better since you've been in the U.S."

"Not really. No machine guns, but living with my father is like living under house arrest. We can't make even the slightest move without his permission. When I hear about your life, Lois, I'm wild with jealousy. I've never been able to bop around in my own car, never been able to just fool around at malls, never gone shopping alone. My mother doesn't dare to express an opinion that hasn't been cleared first. She has to have friends cleared, too.''

"That sounds awful," I said. "Ms. Trainor thinks you'll be a good influence on me. How do you stay so thin? Is it genetic?"

"Not at all. I'll tell you the truth if you promise to keep the secret."

"Of course I will."

"I've just stopped eating. And if I accidentally over-eat, I make myself throw up. It's not hard once you get used to it. My father has always preferred my sister because she's prettier and thinner. So I'm going to lose twenty-five pounds by Thanksgiving as a present to him."

"Are you joking?"

"No, not at all."

"Are you crazy?"

"I don't think so."

"But, Julie, you don't look as if you weigh more than about a hundred and ten."

"Exactly!"

"You'll look sick if you lose twenty-five pounds."

"No, I won't. I'll finally look good enough for him."

"It sounds to me as if you're anorexic."

"Don't be silly. Of course I'm not. I can start to eat anytime I wish."

It was her secret so, of course, I didn't say anything, but I felt that I was a lot better off without a real father than with one like Julie's. What good is life without freedom?

I thought nostalgically about all the things that used to bother me, like Sharon's cronies and employees coming in and out of the house, the chaos and lack of privacy in which I had always lived, and I felt a little homesick. It was as if Julie and I represented two opposite ends of a pole. I'd had too much freedom, and she'd not had enough.

Chapter Twenty-Three

I really lucked out with Julie. I'd thought I could never find another good friend like Paula, and yet I had. We never stopped talking. Neither one of us had ever had a real boyfriend and, to my surprise, when I told her about Jeff she laughed with a lovely, melodious, tinkling laugh and said, "I feel sorry for him. To lose a good friend for such a silly little career." Her amusement took away all of the residual hurt.

It fascinated me to see how different we were. She acted as if she were still living at home. Every single day she got up at six and ran a couple of miles. When she returned, she showered and washed her hair and sat down to study. By the time I struggled up at eight, she'd already accomplished a lot.

Every hour was accounted for. She took riding lessons and tennis lessons and language lessons and swam endless laps in the pool. I admired what she was and everything she did, but even so, I was uneasy with it. It seemed to me that you had to give the body fuel for all that activity, and she was thinner every week. She'd even stopped getting her period. Ms. Trainor called me in once a week to talk about *my* weight, but nobody seemed to notice what was happening to Julie. I thought she looked awful.

Despite my promise, I finally decided to say something. I made an appointment with Ms. Trainor, who wrinkled up her nose at the sight of me as if I smelled bad.

"I'm worried about Julie," I told her. "I think she's too thin. She doesn't eat enough."

"I suggest, Lois, that you worry about your own appearance. There's nothing wrong with Julie. She's lean and muscled, a good athlete. Just worry about yourself. That's a *big* enough job." I stomped furiously out of her office.

"Please eat a lot of turkey," I begged Julie when I kissed her goodbye for Thanksgiving.

When I got home, I found a wonderful surprise. Sharon and Eric had decided not to move. They'd looked at dozens of houses and been unable to find one as beautiful as ours. "We've talked about it a lot," Sharon told me, "and I think Eric trusts me enough to realize that I'll never act as if he's living in my house."

"Oh, Mom. I'm really thrilled. I never wanted to leave."

Missy had bought a condo on Beverly Glen that she loved. "I never realized how wonderful it would be to have my own place," she enthused. "I'm a woman of property. It makes me proud."

The only thing I wasn't so happy about was Paula. We used to be able to talk about everything, and I had looked forward to telling her about school and Julie and my classes. But she had changed. She was interested in only two topics. Weight and boys!

She had joined a diet center and had to go there every day before school to be weighed. She looked really wonderful and, she sheepishly told me, she was going out with Kevin.

"You mean that spas who was so mean to us at the movies?"

"He's changed. Really, Lois. He's completely different."

"You mean maybe he's acting different. But he's still the same person who baited us for being fat."

"I'd rather not discuss it if you don't mind. You'll just have to take my word for it, Lois. He was just kidding around in the movies that time, and he's really a lot of fun."

She told me every detail of every one of their dates and also every boring detail of the lectures she'd attended at the diet place.

"You can never stop thinking about dieting," she burbled away, "but it's worth it. Every morning I sit and meditate on my body. Then I read all sixteen of the diet chants aloud. I do it three times a day. I affirm my ability to eat under optimum conditions."

"I honestly can't believe this is you I'm listening to," I said. "You sound as if you've been brainwashed by the Moonies or some kind of cult. It's just plain boring."

"I'm not going to let you upset me, Lois, just because I've started to care about the right things. It's important to have a boyfriend and it's important to eat right. No matter what you say, it isn't healthy to be obese. I want to listen to my body. My body tells me when it's full and I stop eating.''

I couldn't get her off the subject of weight. She nodded toward Sharon. ''Your mother is getting plump,'' she said.

Sharon sat cuddled in the circle of Eric's arm, her head against his shoulder. She looked so happy and contented that my heart soared with pleasure.

''It's a shame to let herself go,'' Paula continued. ''She'll begin to look as bad as my mother.''

''I don't think Sharon's let herself go. I think she's found herself. I love the way she looks now, kind of soft and friendly instead of brassy and angular. And I also happen to love everything about your mother, including her looks. So please don't say she looks bad. I think that what she is is more important than how she looks.''

Paula spent the rest of our time together telling me about a new way of exercising with industrial-strength rubber bands. She never got around to asking me one thing about my life at school.

I left early the next morning to drive back, anxious to share Thanksgiving experiences with Julie. But when I got there, her room was dark and empty. Her clothes were gone from the closet and dressers. Worried, I ran to Ms. Trainor's office and burst in. She looked at me in horror.

''How dare you enter without knocking? What appalling manners!''

''Where's Julie?''

''I will not speak to you until you enter the proper way. Go back outside and knock.''

I plumped myself down firmly on the couch. ''Of all the silly nonsense. Manners at such a time. Where's Julie?''

With a shrug of distaste, she finally answered, "She's been delayed. She'll be back in a week or so."

Terribly disappointed, I went back to my room. I had never felt more lonely. Julie had been such a wonderful friend that I'd hardly bothered with anyone else. And now there was no one else to talk to. Gradually I tried to cheer myself up. It's only a week, I told myself. Just put in a lot of time studying and it will go quickly.

But she was still not back by the following Sunday, and I was getting anxious about the situation. I had not seen her for almost three weeks. I went to Ms. Trainor's office, remembering this time to knock.

"I have to talk to Julie," I said. "Is she coming back today?"

"I'm afraid not. I don't know when she'll be back. Julie is not well. She's in the hospital."

"What hospital? Where?"

"St. Francis in San Francisco. But she's not receiving phone calls."

"I'm not calling her. I'm going there."

"You can't go there. She's not having any visitors, and you do not have permission to leave this campus."

Without another word, I turned my back and ran to my car. It took me two hours to get to San Francisco and another hour to find the hospital. To my surprise, I had no trouble getting in to see Julie. I simply asked at the desk for her room number and the attendant handed me a card without even looking up.

I shivered going up in the elevator. Hospitals always have a sad, strange antiseptic smell to them, and a nurse was also in the elevator, wheeling an unconscious person on a gurney. It's depressing to see so many sick people in one place, even if that place is trying to help them to get better.

I got off at Julie's floor and found her room. Nobody else was in the room, so I walked in and then stood stock-still trying not to cry. Julie was being fed intravenously from a bag hanging on a stand beside her bed. She looked like a ghost, or a faded Polaroid photograph of the girl I'd known. Her long dark hair was the only spot of color on the bed.

She was the thinnest real person I'd ever seen, as small and thin as a seven-year-old girl. Suddenly, the sight of her triggered a bad memory, and I remembered the pictures of a starving Ethiopian that Missy had hung on the refrigerator door.

Forcing myself to put on an encouraging smile, I tiptoed to the bed and knelt beside it so that my face was level with hers.

"Julie," I whispered.

At the sound, she opened her eyes and smiled at me weakly. "Lois," she said, and a few tears slid effortlessly down her cheeks. "I knew you'd come. I'm so glad to see you." Her voice was as disembodied and fragile as her appearance.

"What's wrong with you?" I asked, digging my nails into the palms of my hands so I wouldn't cry. I pulled a chair up next to the bed and took her hand.

"You were right," she whispered. "I am anorexic."

"Oh, Julie dear. I'm so sorry. So when do you get better? When do you come back to school?"

"I don't know. Not until I put on some weight."

"So start to eat. Eat the way I do. You have to hurry back. School won't be the same without you. Suppose they try to put a different person in your room. Eating's easy. I don't even have to think about doing it."

"I'm going to try. I promise. Just as soon as I'm a little stronger and they take this awful needle out of my arm. And don't worry about a different roommate. We paid for the year, so I'm sure they'll just leave the room empty until I get back. My parents are kind of angry, so they won't do anything to upset me more.''

Her face was so translucent that I thought I could see the bones beneath the skin. And her lips were also devoid of color, more blue than red. She was beginning to fade out. ''Thanks for coming, Lois. You're the first real best friend I ever had. I'm going to sleep now.''

She closed her eyes, and I tiptoed out of the room and stood in the hall crying. And along with my sadness, I felt tremendous anger welling up in me. It was all this insane emphasis on weight that had done her in. Thin as she was, she had suffered from exactly the same concerns as I. I pulled Paula's diet center flyer from my pocket and crumpled it up. They meant well and they were helping Paula, and probably lots of other people, but I didn't want to follow those rules. I didn't want to follow anybody's rules. I didn't want to be forced to think about weight. I was sick and tired of the whole subject.

I wanted to be accepted just the way I was. In the whole history of the world there weren't two people who had the same exact fingerprints. So why should people have to conform to the same ideal weight?

And now Paula, too, was obsessed with weight. She used to be so much fun to talk to, but now she had become boring because of all the diet stuff. She had spent half an hour telling me about four dietetic ways to prepare trout.

It was like that movie *Invasion of the Body Snatchers*. The weight fanatics came from outer space and took over. People's interests were being taken away and replaced with this dumb obsession about weight and jogging and aerobics and Nautilus.

I wasn't going to put up with it much longer. I started to think about what I could do.

Chapter Twenty-Four

To my surprise, when I got back to school, Ms. Trainor didn't even reprimand me. In my innocence, I thought perhaps she had forgiven me for dashing off that way because of my honest concern for Julie.

During the rest of that semester, I buried myself in my work. I really loved learning there. There's something to be said for small classes. It seems easier to go deeply into the subject matter. My favorite subject was Greek civilization. I read everything written by Edith Hamilton and learned wonderful Greek myths about Sisyphus and Tantalus and Prometheus. I decided that I would major in Greek civilization and archaeology in college.

The fact that I liked my studies helped to keep me happy and optimistic while I waited for Julie to return. The other girls were okay, but some people just get under your skin and become part of you and others don't, no matter how much you try. I was sure she'd be there when I returned from Christmas vacation.

I had just finished packing and loading up my car when Ms. Trainor sent for me. I was sure she was going to tell me some good news about Julie or congratulate me on my grades. Instead, without preliminaries, she announced, "I have sent a letter to your mother informing her that we will not be asking you back next semester."

I was so shocked that all I could ask in a strangled voice was, "Why?"

"I'm afraid you're just not the right image for our school."

"But I love it here. I'm a straight-A student."

"You will remember that we only admitted you provisionally to begin with. You promised Mrs. Vance to lose some weight. I've seen no change in your avoirdupois. In addition to your appearance, however, your behavior is unacceptable. There's a stubborn streak in you, Lois, that is wrong for this school. It seems apparent that you have never been disciplined or learned to follow rules. You think it's perfectly all right to do what you like and say what you like and that's not appropriate for our standards. I'm certain that your mother will be able to find a school that's more in keeping with your upbringing."

Half of me wanted to tell her to shove it and march out. But the other half of me remembered how much I loved the classes, the campus, the natural beauty, the peaceful environment. And besides, I wanted to wait for Julie.

"I could try to lose weight and be more disciplined. I did try, but I could try harder."

When she didn't answer, I persisted. "What about my grades? Isn't that important to you?"

"It's only half the story. The sound mind in the sound body!"

I was getting angry. "But if I had the right body and an unsound mind you wouldn't throw me out, would you?"

She looked at me with her usual expression, which combined disgust and annoyance and the intimation that I smelled bad. Which I never did! I was extra careful because of my weight to be neat and clean and shiny.

"I am not here to debate with you, Lois. You will have to excuse me now. I have other appointments. And please, my word is final. No letters or phone calls. You will never fit the Radclyffe School image."

Close to tears but still punching, I said, "I think all this emphasis on image is wrong. I saw poor Julie in the hospital. She was thin enough for you. She was so thin that she looked like a wafer. Are you telling me that fits the image?"

"Julie was a very fine girl. She was a lady."

Something about the way she said that frightened me. "What do you mean, 'was'?"

"Julie passed away last week."

I sat there in total shock for a few seconds, then bolted and ran to my room where I vomited over and over again. Then, filled with sorrow, crying all the way, I drove home. A whole week that dear Julie hadn't been in the world, and I hadn't even known. It was too terrible even to think about.

I tried to hide my unhappiness until after Sharon's wedding. When she asked me about my expulsion, I pretended I didn't care and would be glad to get back to Paula and Beverly Hills High School. She and Eric were so joyous, so glowing, so filled with good humor and goodwill that I just couldn't do anything to bring them down.

They had a great little wedding on our lawn and then flew to Cabo San Lucas, at the tip of Baja California, for a one-week honeymoon.

As soon as they were gone, I dropped my mask and let depression envelop me. All during the Christmas vacation I lay beside my pool and mourned. Paula was there with me every day, just sitting beside me and reading, letting me be alone when I wanted and giving me company when I needed it.

I felt sorry that I'd been so critical of her at Thanksgiving, and I was glad I'd never said anything to her. If I wanted people to be tolerant of me, I had to also be tolerant of other people.

It didn't matter if Paula was totally immersed nowadays in dieting and Kevin. She had a good, loving heart, and that's all that really matters between friends. Probably there were a lot of things about me that annoyed *her*.

After some of the pain of Julie's loss abated, I was ready to take revenge. I told Paula about it. "I'm going to form an organization of fat girls," I told her. "Will you help me with it?"

"Like get serious! Who would want to belong to an organization of fat girls? Nobody wants to be fat. And especially not me. If you want to show up that mean headmistress, join my diet center and get thin. That's the thing to do."

"No," I said. "I want acceptance on my terms, not on hers."

"Then my answer is still no thanks. I want to belong to popular groups of thin girls, not fat girls. I can't feel good about myself unless I'm thin. And besides, Kevin and I kind of belong to a group of couples together. Don't feel bad about that. You're still my best friend, Lois. One of these days you'll find someone, too. I hope you're not angry. Are you?''

"No," I said, trying hard to mean it. "I want you to have the same freedom I would want for myself."

I went ahead without her. I designed a flyer and had a hundred printed. The heading, in tall black letters, said, Fat Power Is Here. The text, on a yellow background below, said:

A Message To All Fat Girls.

Are you tired of being a second-class citizen? Are you tired of being made to feel like a freak? Are you tired of being told you're neurotic? Are you tired of failing at each new fad diet? Are you tired of hearing boys snicker at you? Are you tired of trying to ignore insulting remarks from absolute strangers? If you are, ask yourself this:

Are you any smarter if you wear a size-eight dress? Is your character better if you weigh less? Is your ethical instinct better if you weigh less? Will your name go down in history if you forgo that piece of cake and settle for celery sticks? Do you owe being thin to the world? NO, NO, NO.

Fat Power is here to tell you that who you are and what you are has nothing to do with your dress size. You are neither smarter nor dumber, better nor worse than someone who wears a smaller size jean. No matter what you weigh, you are a human being who is entitled to the same love and respect as your thinner sisters.

To join Fat Power, meet at 8381 Trousdale Place on January 10 from 4-6 p.m.

At last your time has come.

Stop apologizing. You don't owe a thin body to the world. Your body is your business. Yours and yours alone. Fat Girls Fight Back. Fat Power! Fat Power! Fat Power!

I drove all over L.A., from Hancock Park to Santa Monica, putting my signs up in supermarket and food-shop windows. The supermarkets didn't care. They have all kinds of freakish signs up.

When small shopkeepers asked, "What's in it for me?" I told them.

"There are an awful lot of fat people in this city. And they're all going to be interested in which stores help us to get started. We're going to print a brochure of places friendly to fat people, and this store will be on that list. So put up the sign! It's only common sense! Think of all the free publicity! Thousands of new customers!" Not one shop owner refused me.

When Missy came to work the next day, I told her about my plan and enlisted her aid. "You have less and less work to do for Sharon, and there's nobody in town with better organizational skills than you. We'll make you the first executive director of Fat Power. You'll be the only paid employee as soon as we collect dues and have some money."

She was absolutely delighted. "I've been wondering how I would fill my spare time. It's hard to pick up hobbies at my age, after a lifetime of not having them. All right, Lois, I accept the position."

She immediately got on the phone to do PR for the first meeting and to get all of the reporters and television crews out.

"It's kind of a strange feeling—" she beamed at me "—to be doing for you now what I've spent my life doing for Sharon."

"There's something else I want to do, Missy. After I get this organization launched, I intend to sue that Radclyffe School and Ms. Trainor personally. That should give the organization even more publicity."

"I'm with you, Lois. All the way! That school had some nerve kicking you out. I bet you were the smartest girl there. I'll start to think about lawyers."

"Ms. Trainor is going to be very, very sorry," I told her. "I'm not just going to avenge myself. It's also for Julie. I have just begun to fight."

The more action I took, the better I felt about myself.

Chapter Twenty-Five

When Sharon and Eric came back from their honeymoon, we told them about the proposed meeting.

"I thought we were going to lead a private life from now on," Sharon complained.

"Just this first meeting," I pleaded. "I didn't know where else to hold it. But after this we'll alternate homes. Once we have enough money, we'll rent a regular meeting place."

"But what about all of my new plantings?" Sharon moaned.

"Nothing will happen to them," Missy assured her. "She may not even get ten girls. She only had a hundred flyers printed. If she gets even ten percent of her flyers, it would be an unprecedented return. I figure it will take six months to a year of publicity to get her little group rolling."

Was she ever wrong! On the afternoon of the meeting, there were two hundred fat girls and women in our backyard, and cars were parked all the way down Trousdale, practically to Sunset Boulevard. We didn't have enough chairs, so people had to sit on the grass, but nobody seemed to mind. People just seemed glad to be there.

Sharon looked out at the assemblage in shock. "I just don't believe it," she said. "My plantings will be ruined."

"An idea whose time has come," Missy murmured, equally incredulous.

At four o'clock sharp I stood up to speak and held up my hand for silence. I looked out at the group, smiled and said, "Welcome, sisters."

Before I could continue, a mighty cheer went up that lasted for two minutes and gave me gooseflesh up and down my arms.

Paula hadn't come and that made me very sad but, to my delight, Mrs. Lawrence came. She was our first speaker. After the audience grew quiet again, I introduced her as the world-famous opera star, and she began to speak. She told the hushed audience about how she'd almost lost her voice from dieting.

Then she held up pictures of famous fat opera stars like Lauritz Melchior, Kirsten Flagstad, Jessye Norman and Luciano Pavarotti. "All that should matter is the voice," she said. "A rock star can look like a scrawny, scurvy, pockmarked British seaman, but an opera star cannot be fat. Why?"

This audience was as enchanted as her past opera audiences. Then someone cried out, "Sing for us. Please sing for us," and the others took up the cry and begged,

"Sing! sing!" until she graciously agreed to sing a cappella, "Sometimes I Feel Like a Motherless Child."

When she was finished, there wasn't a dry eye on the lawn. Yes, I thought. That was the right song to sing. So many of us were made to feel like motherless, unloved children, so much of the time.

"And now," I told the audience, "I present to you Sharon Long, the famous movie star for twenty-five years, who has just retired from the screen."

The audience went crazy. The posters had shown clearly that the meeting would be held at an exclusive address, but no one could have predicted that real-life, honest-to-goodness celebrities would attend. Most fat girls are accustomed to associating with losers.

Although she still couldn't be called fat in ordinary terms, for a movie star Sharon had become fat. But she had never been more happy and serene. I could have popped with pride.

She stood before them, still beautiful and glamorous, and not the slightest bit concerned about her added weight. She spoke about how she'd agonized all her life about her weight, about the paradox of making so much money and yet going to sleep hungry every night, about the terrible, consuming fear of looking fat on the screen.

"I spent my life worrying about image," she said. "I was convinced that I would instantly lose my career if I put on weight. And I was also sure that no man could love me if I were heavy."

"That's still the way it is," someone called from the audience. Every fat girl understood that fear.

"I've just put on twenty pounds, and for the first time in my life, I feel wonderful. I'm out from under the burden of having to please the world. I no longer belong to the world. The only people I owe anything to are my daughter, my friend, Missy, and my husband. And they love me fat or thin. That's the only kind of love that matters. And I've also finally been able to give up smoking."

The audience gave her a standing ovation while the photographers snapped away. In honesty, I have to make one point here. Sharon really could not compare herself to any of us there. So she now weighed a hundred and thirty. Big deal! She was still probably a size eight, or maybe a ten. But it was very important to the audience to see that even famous movie stars suffered from weight problems that were identical to theirs.

I was the final speaker that day. I stood up, looked out at my sisters and felt so choked with emotion that it took me a few seconds to get started. Nobody who wasn't like us could possibly understand how awful it had always been, how alone we had always felt. But we never would again.

I began to speak, pouring out all the feelings that had been accumulating for over sixteen years. "I've been mocked, starved, reviled, pummeled, exercised, hypnotized, analyzed and made to feel self-indulgent and inferior all my life. I've had to be my own best friend, but even that was hard to do because society told me nobody would want to be friends with a fat girl. Everywhere I turned I felt the same contempt. Once, when I went to the doctor with a wrist I'd just broken roller-skating, he had the nerve to lecture me on injuries that fat people get.

"I've been insulted every day of my life and expected to act a certain way about these insults. How have I been expected to act when people have said terrible things to me? Tell me?"

The audience roared back the correct answer, "Like a good sport."

"Exactly. Like a good sport. Like a cheerful good sport. All the adjustments had to be made by the victims, not by the victimizers. Fat people have had to pretend that insults didn't really hurt. One boy in my school used to go into a whole pig act of snorting, saying 'oink, oink,' and making disgusting noises whenever he saw me. I had to be a good sport. I had to join in the laughter directed against me.

"That boy was covered with zits. Did anybody make mean comments because of that? No, everybody stepped gingerly around him and pretended that he didn't have them. But nobody thinks they have to step gingerly around fat people.

"No, we have had to act like good sports. But that kind of acting is over from now on.

"So we have a mission, a mission to make every fat person in the world feel better, a mission to remind the world that we're human beings with the same feelings and sensitivities as anyone else. And the first thing we're going to do is picket people who make us feel bad. We're not going to let anything pass, not on television, not in the movies, not anywhere.

"When someone makes an unkind remark, we'll catch him up on it. We're going to start to educate people.

"And we're going to reach out to other fat people. When you see a fat, lonely, unhappy girl, dragging miserably around a mall, you're going to walk up to her, smile, shake her hand, give her one of our flyers and say, 'Hello, sister! Fat Power.' After a while we'll have buttons to give away and brochures, too.

"We're going to insist high schools let anybody who wants to, try out for the cheerleading team. And if they tell a fat sister she can't apply because she's overweight and it would spoil their image, we're going to picket that school.

"We're going to write to department stores and insist every one of them have an attractive department for fat girls, not stuck off somewhere in a basement, but in a pleasant, convenient location with extra-big dressing rooms. And we're going to insist they carry a large stock of clothes in any colors we want.

"We're going to publish a magazine to unify us and make us feel better about life and to zap people who put us down. We're going to give free publicity to shopkeepers who are nice to us and to restaurants with chairs big enough for us so that we don't have to sit sideways to eat. We're going to ask that airlines set aside a few seats on every flight for fat people. Lots of fat people don't travel because they can't fit in the seats. If they can put in wheelchair ramps for disabled people, they can put in a few big, comfortable seats for us. And one of these days we're also going to get on the subject of stewardesses. Why whould somebody have to be thin to serve a TV dinner on a plane? If someone can fit down the aisle, that should be good enough. Stewardesses have been fired in the past for putting on weight. We're not going to let that happen in the future.

"We're going to become national, international, and then take Fat Power to other planets. We're going to remind every single person in this country that pluralism means acceptance for all kinds of different sizes. We're going to proudly proclaim to the world that we're not going to let anybody make us feel inferior any longer. We're going to remind the world that our feelings are exactly like theirs."

I held up my fist and shouted, "Fat Power."

"Fat Power," the audience roared back. "Fat Power! Fat Power! Fat Power!"

Sharon put her arms around me. "That's one of the best speeches I've ever heard. I'm proud to be your mother."

Before people left, we decided on a membership fee of ten dollars because a lot of fat people are poor. One woman stood up to say that she was fat because she ate such poor, cheap food. She could not afford the fruits and meats that would keep her slim.

And we kind of elected officers. I became president by acclamation, and the other officers were people who volunteered, including Sharon and Mrs. Lawrence, and then we unanimously elected them. And when I told the group about Missy, they unanimously elected her the paid director.

At the end of the meeting, we arranged to also have the next meeting at my house until we could find a meeting place. And we gave every woman a hundred announcements to distribute.

We ended promptly at six, as I had said on the brochure, and Missy and I stood at the garden exit saying goodbye. Now that I could see the audience individually, I could see they ranged in age from my age to fifty. Some of them were probably older. One of them, who looked about sixty, took my hands in hers and pressed them to her lips.

"God bless you," she said, squeezing my hands. "You've given me hope for the first time in my life."

I started to cry, and then we cried together.

Chapter Twenty-Six

After that, everything began to snowball. Thanks to Missy's expertise with public relations, the next day the story of our meeting was all over the *L.A. Times*. She took five of the women who'd volunteered at our meeting and arranged for them to set up similar meetings at ten spots within a two-hundred-mile radius of L.A. Sharon and I drove to each of those meetings, giving essentially the same speeches as at the first one, and at the end of the first month we had a thousand members and ten thousand dollars to plow right back into expenses.

Missy hired a staff, found an office where she and the staff could work and where we could also hold our L.A. meetings, and then, after covering the entire state, south to north, she began to move to other states. Sharon and I began to fly to some meetings, and Mrs. Lawrence took over others.

Missy rented a large computer and hired people to computerize our operation. None of us could really believe what was happening. It was as if we'd unleashed a flood.

The following week I hired a team of Beverly Hills lawyers and called a press conference to announce that we were suing the Radclyffe School because it had expelled me. My lawyers hoped it would be a landmark case in fat discrimination. Yippee!

I think it was that news conference that really put us over the top. First it was just a news item on the evening news and then, in the next few days, Sharon and I were on all of the morning news shows and eventually on *Donahue*.

The next six months were really crazed. Missy and her staff took over three floors of an office building, we incorporated, we developed a hundred chapters and we had to hire additional staff to answer the letters that were coming in from all over the country. I was hired to put together a book called *Confessions of Fat Girls* which was supposed to be interviews with many of our members, and Sharon and I spoke and founded groups in London and Berlin.

On the day we returned from Paris, Missy had great news for us. The Radclyffe School had agreed to publicly apologize and take me back, if I liked. "Do you want to go back?" Sharon asked.

"No. But I hope this sets some kind of precedent."

"So how are you feeling?" Eric asked with a hug. "You'll go down in history. Triumphant?"

"You'd better believe it. In one year I've gone from being a public embarrassment to receiving a public apology and becoming a media star."

The four of us toasted one another with champagne and hugged and kissed. It was one of those superbly sweet moments that doesn't come too often, so you have to recognize and treasure it when it does.

None of us could have foreseen what would happen to me at the end of six months of madly hectic racing around. I had always avoided scales and had stopped looking at my body years before. But one day Paula came over for a swim, looked at me and gasped.

"Lois," she said. "Have you looked at yourself recently?"

"What do you mean looked at myself? Something awful?"

She grabbed my hand and dragged me in front of the cabana mirror. "Now look," she said.

I looked and my jaw dropped. It was as if I were looking at Sharon instead of myself. The girl who looked back was not only pretty, she was thin.

"Get on the scale," Paula urged with excitement in her voice.

For once I didn't argue. I stood on the scale and watched the needle move. It stopped at a hundred and thirty. I couldn't believe it.

"You get on," I told Paula.

She stepped on. One thirty-five. "Is that what you weigh?" I asked.

"On the button. I was weighed this morning at my diet center. So the scale must be right. You're not fat any longer, Lois. You got thin from all that running around."

That night, Sharon, Eric, Missy and I held a conference. "What are we going to do?" I asked. "I can't keep going around and shouting Fat Power if I look like this."

"I think this has come at the best possible time," Eric said. "In September you have to go back for your last year of high school. You're slender and pretty and a celebrity, so this should be the best year of your life."

"But what about Fat Power?"

"Missy and Sharon and Rosetta Lawrence are having the time of their lives. This is a big business, and it can only keep growing. I suggest that you go back to high school and become a silent partner, and let them run it. When you get out of college, you little baby tycoon, if you change your mind about becoming an archaeologist, you'll have the business to come back to."

"But I thought Sharon was going to retire after you got married. Didn't you want a nonworking little housewife wife?"

"That wasn't what I wanted. And I never asked for it. It was what she wanted. Or thought she wanted. But now that I see how happy she is to be back in the fray, I don't think she ever really wanted to retire. I think she needed a change, a new challenge, and thanks to you, she really has it."

I looked at Sharon and Missy. The old team. "Would that be all right with you two?" I asked.

"Of course," they said together.

"You don't mind sharing Mom with the world, Eric?"

"She shares me with my world, doesn't she?"

"Oh, Eric." I threw my arms around him. "I really love you."

Chapter Twenty-Seven

When I went back to school in September, everybody made a big fuss over me at first, then it died down. After all, our school is full of kids of celebrities and they're all pretty blasé.

Then one day I was walking down the hall at the end of the school day when I saw him. Prince Charming. Blond, blue-eyed, dimpled, reminding me of that betrayer Jeff. I was still a sucker for that kind of looks.

He was standing at his locker, and I did something the old me never would have had the confidence to do. But I had spoken to groups all around the United States and in Europe and I'd been on the *Donahue Show*. I wasn't the fearful, apologetic girl I'd been.

I walked over to his locker, took a deep breath, smiled and said, "Hi. I'm Lois Long. What's your name?"

"Peter Brewer and I just moved here from New York, and I'm so lonely and unhappy that if you say anything nice to me I just might burst into tears."

"I'm going to say 'Welcome,'" I said, tucking my hand into his arm, "but please don't cry. When other people cry, it makes me cry, too."

He laughed. "I don't feel like crying any longer."

"Can I give you a lift?" I asked.

"You sure can. Let me ask you a question."

"Go ahead."

"Do you have a boyfriend?"

I held his arm a little tighter. "Not yet."

He stopped walking, turned and looked down at me. "A little on the skinny side, aren't you?"

"Forget about my weight. I have a great personality."

* * * * *

I must have been asleep for about an hour when I heard it on the door, a soft knock as though the person didn't want to wake up anyone but me.

"Who is it?" I called out in a loud whisper.

I sat as still as I could trying to decide what to do. It wasn't hot in the room, but I could feel a cold sweat on the back of my neck.

What was on the other side of the door? I didn't think it was something I wanted to meet.

Monica's going to find out who or what is lurking behind that closed door. She's in for a real shock!

Read all about it in

SHOCK EFFECT
by
Glen Ebisch

Coming from Crosswinds in November.

COMING NEXT MONTH
FROM

 CROSSWINDS™

SHOCK EFFECT
By Glen Ebisch

Being a waitress in a summer hotel can be more than just hard work, as Monica found out when she discovered a corpse in a bedroom. Was it murder?

KALEIDOSCOPE
By Candice Ransom

Cress and Darien find that life is a mysterious design of changing patterns. After initial misunderstandings, they decide to explore it together.

AVAILABLE THIS MONTH

THE EYE OF THE STORM
Susan Dodson

BIGGER IS BETTER
Sheila Schwartz

COMING NEXT MONTH
FROM
Keepsake